Love's Last Messenger
and other stories

Earl McKenzie

LMH PUBLISHING LIMITED

© 2022 Earl McKenzie
First Edition
10 9 8 7 6 5 4 3 2 1

All rights reserved. No part of this book may be reproduced, stored in a retrieval system, or transmitted, in any form or by any means, electronic, mechanical, photocopying, recording, or otherwise, without the expressed written permission of the publisher or author.

All LMH Publishing Limited titles are available at special quantity discounts for bulk purchases for sales promotion, premiums, fund-raising, educational or institutional use.

This is a work of fiction. Names, characters, places and incidents either are the products of the author's imagination or are used fictitiously, and any resemblance to actual persons, living or dead, events or locales, is entirely coincidental.

Editor: K. Sean Harris
Cover Painting by: Earl McKenzie
Cover Design: Sanya Dockery
Book Design, Layout & Typeset: Sanya Dockery

Published by: LMH Publishing Ltd.
Suite 10-11
Sagicor Industrial Park
7 Norman Road
Kingston C.S.O, Jamaica
Tel: 876-938-0005
Fax: 876-759-8752
Email: lmhbookpublishing@cwjamaica.com
Website: www.lmhpublishing.com

Printed in the U.S.A.   ISBN: 978-976-657-075-0

CATALOGUING-IN-PUBLICATION DATA AVAILABLE AT THE
NATIONAL LIBRARY OF JAMAICA

Contents

The Showers of the Mountains	1
A Gift of Yams	32
Fenkeh-Fenkeh's Triumph	47
Miss Love and Mister Lovemore	51
Love's Last Messenger	61
In the Garden of Her Names	78
The Bull	106
The Retablo	147
Lively Up Yourself	173
Something is Gone	184

for Trudy

The Showers of the Mountains

"They are wet with the showers of the mountains, and embrace the rock for want of a shelter."

THE BOOK OF JOB, 24:8

Lionel

He walked along the newly asphalted road that curved around a grassy spur on the hillside. He used both hands to grip the wooden toolbox that he carried on his left shoulder, and he walked slowly under its weight. The clear white light of the noonday sun shone fiercely on his tanned brown face, and there was a slight squint in his eyes as he resisted it.

As he entered the square at Mount Carlos, he glanced at the closed shop on the ground floor of the large wooden building on his left; his son Mark had opened a leather-shop there that had quickly failed, and the troubled young man had returned to Kingston. He crossed the square and mounted the piazza of the long, wooden shop that was on the eastern side of the square. At its northern end the shoemaker, one of Mark's few customers, was hammering the sole of the shoe he was repairing.

"Hoy Maas Tim!" said Lionel.

"Bless you brother Nello. It seems you knock-off work early today."

"Carpentry in the morning and farming in the afternoon. It is time to reap the corn before bird nyam dem off."

"So you soon have your cornshelling."

"Yes. I will invite you. More time."

"More time, Nello."

Lionel walked along the piazza. There were no customers inside the shop. He stopped at the rumbar at the other end and went inside. The cool interior gave him some relief. He put his toolbox on the floor. Then he took a handkerchief from his pocket, wiped the sweat from his face, and returned the piece of chequered fabric to his pocket. He walked over to the counter and rattled his knuckle on it. "Serve! Serve!" he called out.

The Chinese shopkeeper appeared at the door. He was a small, thin man with shrewd eyes and a kind mouth.

"Missa Lee please serve me a cream soda. I am dying of thirst. What a sun hot! We may get a hurricane this year."

Mr Lee went over to the kerosene-operated fridge on his left, took out the bottled drink, opened it and placed it in front of Lionel. "You want a glass?"

"No," replied Lionel as he raised the bottle to his lips and with big draughts, downed more than half his drink. He returned the bottle to the counter and said, "I could drink another but Hannah is preparing lunch."

"Didn't expect to see you here at this time of the day, Missa Alexander," said Mr Lee.

"My field bear a nice crop of corn this year. I want to start reaping them after lunch."

"Too bad about Mark's shop," said Mr Lee. "In business you have to make sure you have a market for your product before you start. As far as I know we have only about three shoemakers in this part of the island. We Chinese stick to food mostly, for we know that everybody need food. What is Mark doing now?"

"Back in town drinking rum, I hear. He is becoming quite a waterbird. After all the money we spent on him. We batter and batter to send him to one of the best high schools in Kingston. And him don't pass anything."

"What is he good at?"

"Frankly I don't know. I didn't get much schooling myself. Never went beyond A-Class. Just learned enough to write my name. My father never believed in this book-business. He took me out of school to teach me the carpentry that his father taught him. He wanted me to be able to earn a living and help the family, especially since I was their first child."

"We Chinese people believe a lot in education. Our famous philosopher, Confucius, was a great teacher."

"At the time I couldn't see what was in it myself. We had no teachers or parsons in our family. We are not a book-family. But Hannah believed in it. She wanted to learn to play the organ so she could play at church. She wanted to become a teacher or a postmistress. So it was mostly she who pushed Mark. I had my doubts but just went along with it. And the second one, Sidney, is following him in this book-business. He is going to a high school now. And his head is always in a book. Book, book, book!"

Mr Lee stared through the door at the square. "It getting dark all of a sudden. And I can smell rain."

Lionel turned to look outside. "You are right! The rain is good but I hope it don't wash out my plan for the corn."

They heard raindrops sweep across the zinc roof. Lionel turned to leave. The intensity of the rain was increasing.

"You will get wet. Why not wait for it to hold up?" said Mr Lee. "I was just about to cook my lunch. Why don't you come in and finish your drink while I cook?"

Lionel hesitated for a moment. It was not Mr Lee's practice to invite people from the district into his home. His only company was other Chinese men, his fellow shopkeepers, who visited to eat, chat, laugh and gamble. But it would be impolite to say no, so he agreed. Mr Lee pulled up the hinged opening at the end of the counter to let him in. With his unfinished bottle of soda in his hand, Lionel followed him to the back of the shop. Rain was now pounding the roof.

"Have a seat," said Mr Lee as he pointed to a wooden table with four chairs. As Lionel pulled out a chair and sat down, Mr Lee began lighting a charcoal stove on the floor. He opened the cupboard and took out a V-shaped pot that he held up to show Lionel. "This is a wok. It's shaped to keep in the heat so you can cook fast." Using a chopper with a short wooden handle that Lionel had never seen before, he began chopping vegetables quickly and expertly. He lifted a block of yellow substance to show Lionel. "This is beancurd. It is like a cheese made from soymilk. We call it the boneless meat for it is high in protein. I already steamed my rice. Now I am going to make a stir-fry with shrimps."

Lionel watched with fascination as Mr Lee placed the wok on the live coals and began stirring the vegetables in the oil with what looked like a wooden fork, while adding dried shrimps from a packet, and sprinkling what he said was soy sauce. A mouth-watering aroma soon filled the dining room.

"You know how to cook?" he asked Lionel.

"I can't even make a cup of tea. Hannah once gave me directions on how to cook the rice while she went to church. After I poured the rice into the pot and saw it sink to the bottom I gave up! We had canned herring and bread for lunch that Sunday. Hannah was furious! She never asked me to cook again."

"In China every man is expected to be a good cook. The wife does the ordinary cooking but on special occasions, like the Lunar New Year, it is the husband who does the cooking."

As Mr Lee continued preparing his meal, Lionel looked around the small dining room. The walls of unpainted wood that showed their grains were bare except for a calendar with Chinese characters and a picture of Chinese workers wearing hats like inverted woks, standing knee-deep in muddy water, apparently planting rice.

"Would you like some of my lunch?" asked Mr Lee.

"Just a taste, I have to leave space for Hannah's cooking."

Mr Lee stuffed rice into a small bowl and put the rest, what Jamaicans would call 'the watchman', on top of it. He made a smaller version for Lionel and placed it in front of him. Then he sat facing his guest with his own bowl and two pairs of chopsticks.

"Oh my goodness!" said Mr Lee. "I forgot that you may not know how to use chopsticks."

"I most certainly do not," said Lionel.

"And I don't have any knives or forks in the house. I will just have to give you a quick lesson. Or none of my lunch for you."

"I will give them a try," said Lionel.

Mr Lee went over to him and put a pair of the chopsticks between Lionel's right thumb and forefinger, and showed him how to keep a firm grip on one while using the other to grip the food. Lionel laughed at the idea but he kept trying.

"Don't try to lift every single grain of rice with the chopsticks for that is impossible. Do this." He raised his own bowl to right under his mouth and gently shoveled small portions of the food into his mouth.

Lionel ate the food with obvious relish. Then he said:

"This meal is like an ideal marriage. The sauce is in harmony with the rice. And in spite of the heat of the frying, the vegetables are still fresh and crisp. The bean-curd is like a love that absorbs and blends everything around it."

"You are a poet!" said Mr Lee, smiling.

"Cheers!" said Lionel, raising his unfinished bottle of soda.

"Would you like some rice wine so we can make some real toasts?"

"You mean they can use rice to make wine?"

"Chinese can turn anything that grow out of the earth into wine."

"I will try it."

Mr Lee opened a cupboard and pulled out a bottle and two small glasses. He returned to his seat, poured the wine into the glasses and placed one in front of Lionel. Lionel stared at it and reflected that it looked like white rum but with a little more colour. He picked up his glass, raised it and said:

"To the prosperity of you and your shop!"

Mr Lee raised his and said, "To you and your family."

Mr Lee watched as Lionel took a cautious sip, seemed pleased, and then took another. He swallowed his own drink in a single draught.

"How long have you and Hannah been married?"

A slight drumroll of thunder accompanied the rain.

"As you can see, Mark is a grown young man. And his brother Sidney is going to high school."

"I see. How did you and Hannah meet?"

"Her late father was a planter who owned a lot of land and livestock. I used to work for him part-time cutting grass for his animals. He had several pretty daughters and Hannah was the one that caught my fancy. She was tiny, had jet-black hair, and so quiet you would think that butter would not melt in her mouth. I started sweet-talking her trying to bring her out. She seemed interested, and before I knew what I was doing, I fall her."

There was a new look of energy in Mr Lee's eyes, but it was not detected in the matter-of-fact tone with which he replied.

"So you fell her."

"Yes. And when her belly started growing and her parents noticed it, they accosted her and she called my name. I found myself in very deep waters. They were churchgoing people and they saw a pregnant teenage daughter as a blemish on the family-name. They demanded that I marry her." He rubbed his chin as if feeling for his razor bumps.

"But I didn't feel that I was ready for marriage, I told them when they summoned me to their house. I was just getting into my trade, had very little money, couldn't afford to build a house.

"'You should have thought of that before you put a bread in her oven'," said her father, a stern disciplinarian famous for putting a supple-jack whip to the backsides of his children. "He had it stuck behind a rafter in the ceiling, and he glanced up at it as he spoke to me. He was the type who would try to beat a grown man."

There was energy in Mr Lee's eyes once again, but he said nothing, silently indicating by his expression that he was keen on hearing the whole story.

There were two loud claps of thunder.

"My own father took a different attitude. I was their oldest child, and a son, so he liked the idea of starting to have grandchildren. He said: 'If you are man enough to knock her up, you should be man enough to marry and take care of her.' My mother seemed to be in very deep thought about it but said nothing."

"Another drink?" suggested Mr Lee.

"Sure, a bird cannot fly with one wing!"

They both laughed and Mr Lee poured more wine.

"At the bottom of it was the fact that I did not want to be a father. They say all women have a maternal instinct and that all men have a paternal instinct. I love women. And I love other people's children. But I don't seem to have much of that father instinct myself. That is the truth. Make of what you will. I have to live according to what I feel deep in myself."

"You come from a large family?"

"Seven younger brothers and one sister. And I was a kind of second father to them. Perhaps that used up all my fatherhood. What about you?"

"My wife and four children are still in China. One day I will have to decide if I should bring them here, or save my money and go back home."

The thunder lost all its restraint and exploded with claps so powerful they sounded like the Last Judgement.

"But, of course, you did marry her."

"Yes. I am a man who can be led but not driven. I wouldn't let them drive me into it. I waited and thought about it, and married her when I felt that it was the right thing to do."

"Sounds like the rain is holding up," said Mr Lee. "You may be still be able to reap some corn."

"Yes, I better be going."

Mr Lee led the way back into the shop. Lionel lifted his toolbox to his shoulder.

"More time, Missa Lee."

"More time Missa Alexander."

Lionel walked out onto the piazza. He went down the steps carefully to the new wet asphalt that was beginning to glisten in the emerging sunlight. He resumed walking down the road, once more feeling the weight of his toolbox. The air felt cleansed and refreshed.

Hannah

Except for the absence of Lionel, who was now dead and buried in the family plot on the hillside below the house, it was a typical Saturday evening for Hannah. Preferring the outside kitchen to the gas stove that Sidney had bought for them, since she felt that food cooked over a woodfire tasted better, she carefully prepared her Sunday dinner of curried chicken with white rice and boiled green bananas. While the pots were boiling, she washed a salad tomato and some lettuce and placed them in the fridge that Sidney had also given them. Then she made a jug of soursop juice and put it in the fridge.

Then she went outside and picked flowers from her garden. She returned to the living room and placed some of them in the large blue vase, one of their wedding presents, on the centre table. She put the others into a smaller transparent vase she intended to take to church the following morning: since the start of her marriage it had been her custom to take flowers to the Sunday service each week, and place them on the altar before the start of the ceremony.

Following that, she turned on the television that Sidney had bought for them, and she sat and watched it while mending clothes on her lap.

When she started feeling hungry she went into the dining room that Sidney had also added to their small home with money from his first year's salary, and brewed a cup of tea with mint picked from her garden. She sweetened the beverage with wet-sugar and accompanied it with crackers and cheese.

At nightfall, as the chickens began flying to their roosts, she went to bed.

She awoke at dawn and turned on the radio. Its continual flow of services, coming mostly from American evangelists, accompanied her through the ringing of her church-bell a mile away; her breakfast of saltfish fritters, harddough bread and hot homemade chocolate; her bath in the bathroom that Sidney had employed a carpenter to add to the house; and getting dressed in her bedroom. She would wait for the arrival of Miss Evelyn, her best friend, fellow widow, and walking partner to and from church on Sundays.

"Nana! Nana! You ready?" she finally heard Miss Evelyn calling from the yard.

"Coming Lyn! Mi soon come!" She powdered her face, and stood for a while examining her reflection in the mirror on her wardrobe. The small brown woman with the sad eyes, wearing a black hat with matching dress and shoes that looked back at her, was not someone she had ever imagined seeing there. At least not with that particular wounded look in her eyes. She took her bible, hymnbook from the bedside table, stuffed them into her handbag, and headed for the living room. She opened the front door and greeted Miss Evelyn who was standing in the yard, tall with a dignified reserve, her white hat and matching dress contrasting dramatically with her dark skin and black handbag and shoes.

Hannah handed her the handbag. "Please hold these for me while I get the flowers and lock the door."

Those tasks completed, she retrieved her handbag and joined Miss Evelyn in the yard.

"Di roses pretty," said Miss Evelyn.

"All my flowers flourishing because of the rain."

In the brilliant sunshine, the two elegantly dressed and sweetly perfumed women began walking towards the main road. Beside her tall friend, Hannah seemed even more petite. They turned and began walking south towards the small church that was barely visible against the dark-green hillside in the distance.

A few minutes later, they turned from the main road onto the parochial one that pedestrians preferred: it was in the shadow of a long hill and sheltered from the heat of the rising sun, had less traffic, was lined with fields and orchards, had dramatic views of western valleys, and its unpaved surface and soft soil was easier to walk on. At the bottom of the first gradient, Hannah stopped at the gate of her old family home. Sheets of rusty zinc from its roof were strewn on the trees below. The surviving grey walls were showing signs of erosion. The two women stood side by side and looked down at the signs of the vandalism.

"Mt Carlos not like what it used to be," said Miss Evelyn.

"It is now hard to believe that I spent most of my childhood in that house. We got married in a booth in that yard. My parents and two of my brothers are buried down there. I left it when I married Lionel and we moved into our own house on the other side of the hill." Hannah began walking away.

"How old were you when you got married?"

"Twenty. I was only seventeen when he put me in the family way and that Satan refused to marry me. Three years of disgrace in my churchgoing family and in the eyes of the community. That was how I started my life as a woman in this world."

"He only wanted to blow off his steam, not make a baby. What kind of husband was he? I remember him as a pleasant and jokify man."

"That was what drew me to him. He was good-looking sweet-mouth, sang and played the guitar, and was a great dancer. All that changed the moment he discovered that I was pregnant. From that day on I started seeing a different man. That said, he was a good provider. When he got his pay he gave me every penny, and I gave him back some for his pocket money to have a few drinks with his friends. I took care of all the family finances. He had no sense of money."

"What was he like as a father?"

"That was his downfall. Mark was born and raised in my parents' home."

"What? A young couple not raising their firstborn child in their home?"

"Lionel did not want that child. He never bonded with him. But his grandparents clearly loved him, so we let him live with them. We gave them money for his food, clothes, books and school fees."

Hannah stopped walking and looked up into the branches of the big naseberry tree on their right. "This was the garage where my father parked his truck. We children used to play in its ruins. If you look carefully, you can still see marks of the iron dust in the soil."

"He used to be a fairly well-off man, wasn't he?"

"He owned land and employed plenty people. I wanted him to give me a better education but he wasn't interested in that. He had a lust for land and couldn't wait to buy another piece. It seems it was the only thing that gave him a sense of security in the world. But when he died and it was divided up for his many children and grandchildren, each of us got a small piece and found ourselves poor." She resumed walking and Evelyn fell into stride with her.

"When Mark left the elementary school, where he passed nothing, we sent him to a good high school in Kingston. He boarded with one of my sisters. l was reluctant to spend all that money on him, but I managed to pressure him to go along with it. Again, Mark didn't pass anything and took to drink and bad company."

"Did you see him often during that time?"

"No. He came to visit me once and was well-dressed and well-spoken. Sidney was at school that day and didn't see him. Lionel was at work. A few years later he brought his lady, a woman who looked older than me. I went to Kingston to visit the used car dealer where he worked. They repaired and sold cars, and his job was to go and seize them when the people didn't pay up. It was a job that took him all over the island. Sidney was at the university by then, and I told him where Mark lived and urged him to visit his brother. He told me that he did."

"Did they become close?"

"No. They barely knew each other. Another of my thorns, my dear. Three months after Lionel died they found Mark dead in his room after one of those trips to the country to bring back a car. Sidney took charge of his funeral. The last thing Mark said to me was that he would soon come back to visit me. He came back in his coffin. We gave him a home funeral, and I remember that you were there. He is now buried at his father's feet. I want to be buried beside him."

"Not beside Lionel?"

"No. Beside Mark."

At the end of the long ridge on their left, the parochial road reconnected with the main one. The sun was now higher in the sky and its heat hit them hard. Both women took their umbrellas from their handbags and raised them, Miss Evelyn a pink one and Hannah a black one. With the increased likelihood of traffic, they walked on the right side of the road to face oncoming automobiles.

"My husband Trevor was a postman for forty years," said Miss Evelyn, "and he walked this road every weekday in the hot sun with the big canvas bag on his back. And there were at least two women on his route that he couldn't resist, so he sired two outside children with them."

"How do you feel about that?"

"Is so man stay."

"I heard one rumour that a woman, a shopkeeper, once tried to seduce Lionel one night after she closed her shop, but I don't know if he yielded to her. In this country you should believe half of what you see and none of what you hear. So I have chosen not to believe it. But except for a stint as a farmworker in America, and I don't know what he did over there, he came home late every night. But he came home. For 57 years."

"I remember that Sidney came as a bit of a surprise to you and everybody."

"Yes. He was born fourteen years after Mark. Imagine that. But he was a child I prayed for. Is a prayed-for baby that."

"I have four grandchildren, but I never hear you talk about any?"

"Two boy pickney and not a single grandchild. I don't know what make of that. It must mean something, but what?"

"That is too deep for me."

They were approaching the village where the church was located. They greeted a few persons they knew. Then they began climbing the gradient up to the church. As they entered the building Hannah went up and placed her vase of flowers on the altar. She closed her eyes and her lips moved as she prayed quietly, ending with the words, "And forgive us our trespasses as we forgive them that trespass against us." She retraced her steps to sit beside Miss Evelyn.

After the hymns, readings and listening to a sermon about the parable of the Prodigal Son, they began walking back home. Apart from mundane things about cooking, sewing and planting, they said very little to each other. They felt that the weight of the morning's exchanges were enough.

"Why don't you come and have dinner with me?" said Hannah when they arrived at her gate.

"I would love to, Nanah, but some of Trevor's relatives coming to spend the afternoon with me and I have to get ready for them. Next time."

"More time, then," said Hannah as she turned into the entrance.

She changed into more comfortable clothes. Then she warmed her dinner in the gas oven. She ate at the dining table, remembering Lionel and Sidney having long conversations there while the father told the son stories about old-time days at Mt Carlos. Mark never dined there.

After the meal she went into her bedroom and stretched out on the bed. She reflected that during the final years of their marriage, and Lionel's worsening illness, it had become her bed alone, for he had slept in Sidney's bed in the adjoining room. After calling for her assistance late one night, she had gone in to help change his pyjamas. When she was finished he said, "Thank you." They were his final words to her. He died that night.

She turned over and laid on her stomach for a while before she fell asleep.

She awoke to the sound of rain pouring on the zinc roof. It was still daylight but she could tell that night was not far off. It would soon be another night alone in the house with only the memories of a departed Lionel and a visiting Sidney. Mark had slept under that roof only once, the night after his father's funeral, but he had opted to sleep alone on the sofa of the living room.

Hannah reached over and pulled her worn bible from her handbag. It was a book that she often told people was her rock. She turned on the bedside lamp and moved closer to it. She began reading her favourite chapter: Romans 8. With the rain thrashing the roof, she read the last chapter aloud:

"For I am persuaded that neither death nor life, nor angels, nor principalities, nor powers, nor things present, nor things to come, nor height, nor depth, nor any other creature, shall be able to separate us from the love of God, which is in Christ Jesus our Lord."

She laid on her back and thought about them while listening to the rain.

Mark

Bald, and wearing a blue pin-striped Kariba suit, he walked into a rum bar in Kingston around 3:30 pm. There were no other customers there. "Hoy Sonny," he said to the East Indian bartender as he sat down at the counter. "The usual."

"Markie, you look like you just saw a ghost," said Sonny. He studied his customer's face carefully, like a boxing referee trying to decide if he should stop the fight.

"Hurry up," said Mark.

Sonny placed a small bottle of overproof white rum and a glass with ice-cubes in front of Mark.

"I am coming from my father's funeral," said Mark.

"Your father! I never heard you talk about your father."

"I hardly knew the man."

"How come?"

Mark poured a drink and took a deep draught, after which he clasped the bottle in his hand as if it were his greatest treasure.

"For as long as I knew myself," he said, " home was my grandparents' home. Little by little they told me that a little brown woman who visited us often, and who everybody called Aunt Nanah, was my real mother, and not Granny who was raising me. But Granny has always felt like my real mother. Aunt Nanah, I still call her that, was very nice to me, and I came to see her as my nice Aunt Nanah. And there was a man who everybody called Uncle Nello, who also visited often, and who laughed a lot and cracked jokes, and who Granny one day told me was my real father, and not my Grandpa who was the one I looked up to as such. This Uncle Nello was nice and social to everybody else, but kept a certain distance from me.

"I grew up in that home with two other boys, my cousins. We built and rode a wooden cart up and down the gradient above the house, under a number-eleven mango tree on the parochial road. We made slingshots and hunted birds, bathed in the waterfall on Sunday mornings. We went to the same school where I was good at mental arithmetic but not much else."

"And where were your parents in all of this?"

"Many years later Granny told me that it was they who were paying for my food, clothes and books. And later when they decided to try with me at a technical school here in Kinston, they paid the fees as well. While studying I boarded with my aunt who had a stall at Coronation Market. The only thing I got from that technical school is my love of motor-vehicles. But I didn't pass any exam there either. Everybody got disappointed in me. I started drinking with my friends."

"Do you know why you did not live with them?"

"No. That has remained a mystery to me to this day. Whatever my father's view of that was, he took that with him to his grave today."

"All I know is that I now have a mother."

"You plan to go live with her?"

"Plenty people ask me that at the funeral. But I don't think I will. She couldn't put up with my heavy drinking. But I hope to visit her often. Maybe she will explain a few things to me one day."

"You brought your brother here once for a drink. He drank a beer to your rum. He looked much younger and seems to be a nice guy."

"Sometime in my teens Granny told me that the boy I sometimes saw with my mother was my brother. I was puzzled by that. Why did he live with them and me with my grandparents? As I told you that puzzlement has always been with me. When he passed his exams and got his degrees I saw his name in the newspaper here in town, and I used to show them to my friends and boast about him. He was a star-boy. But I met him only a couple of times. Twice his mother urged him to try and find me, and he came to the rooms where I lived nearby here. Once, while travelling in the country I stopped by the house where he lived. But we never really connected. I knew too little about him and he knew too little about me. We were from the same parents but we lived in two different worlds. People say we both resemble our father. I can't say."

"Is a few years now since your woman died. But you didn't marry her. Any children?"

"I gave up on the young-gal dem and chose an older woman. But I was never one to join any Lodge. I think I breed one of the young-gal down the country. But she married another man shortly after. Dem say her son resemble me a little, so I may have given the poor bastard a jacket. But I don't know for sure. I decided not to press it. Why break up what I hear is a marriage? And he is an engineer and I am a used car salesman. Why would she want to leave him for me."

"How was the funeral?"

Mark emptied the glass, made a face and shook his head right, left, right left. He replenished the glass with rum.

"One of my cousins told me about his death and the date of the funeral. I took a minibus and went up to Mt Carlos. I went straight to my old home at my grandmother's. Both grandparents have long been dead. Only two of my unmarried aunts still live there. The younger one didn't even recognize me. But the other, the oldest daughter and the one with whom I boarded during my schooldays in this city, offered me lunch. I sat alone at the old dining table and ate. People kept coming and going, including one or two of my schoolmates. But most of them were strangers to me now. It started to rain. I went into the living room and sat on the sofa. Photos of some of my uncles and aunts were on the walls. I remembered the old wind-chime made of bamboo and bits of coloured glass that hung from the ceiling, that a wandering grand-uncle I never knew had brought back from his travels overseas. I sat there and remembered my childhood in that old house. And it rained and rained.

"After the rain Sidney arrived at the gate in his car. He owned his own car. He came down to the house looking for me. Me and my former caretaker aunt, now in her senior years, followed him to the car. Our mother was in the passenger seat beside him, and me and my aunt joined his girlfriend in the back seat. We drove to the church in silence.

"I didn't join the family in the mourner's bench in the front. I sat with the rest of the congregation, and near the back. I sat there and heard my father described as a non-churchgoing man who was nevertheless a famous singer at set-ups and nine-nights; as a good carpenter who had helped to make the houses of many in that congregation, and who also made coffins free of charge for bereaved families in the community; as an independent man who loaned but never borrowed; as a humourist who loved few things better than a good joke; and who loved children so much he always carried sweets in his pocket just in case he ran into some of them.

"After the service I was one of the first persons outside. The driver of the hearse was a bit reluctant when I asked him, but when I told him who I was, he allowed me to ride at the back of the hearse at the foot of the coffin, and sitting in that position, I accompanied my father to his burial.

"I intended to spend the night at my old home, but my old aunt who had succeeded my granny as the hostess of the family, explained that the house was full of guests for the night, and went to ask my mother if I could sleep in my real family home for the night. She agreed. Sidney came and escorted me to the home in which he himself had been born and raised.

"But I insisted on sleeping alone on the sofa in the living room. I am a morning-walker. So I woke up early and went for a long walk all around Mt Carlos, noting some of the remembered places of my childhood where we played gigs and marbles and flew kites.

"At midday I returned home and shared lunch with my mother and Sidney. We watched television and chatted a bit. I promised my mother I would visit her soon. I caught the next minibus back to Kingston. And here I am."

Sonny studied Mark's face again with the care of a referee trying to decide if a fighter has had enough. "I am not serving you anymore rum today," he said, stopping the contest. "Go home, have a meal and go to bed."

"You are sounding as if you are my father."

"I have eight children. And although I am a bartender, I don't want any of them becoming rum-heads. Go home, Markie!"

"Yes. I am going to a restaurant and order a bowl of red-peas soup with beef. Then I am going home to sleep. And I will be up bright and early to have my usual long walk around the city. I know this city by heart. People ask me if I am not afraid to walk alone since Kingston not as safe as it used to be. I tell them that the gunmen know me, and they know that I have nothing for them to rob. The gunmen are too smart to rob poor people."

"Go home, Mark," Sonny said gently but firmly.

Mark paid his bill and pocketed the change.

He rose from the chair he knew so well he felt he almost owned it, and began walking towards the exit. Two men met him at the door. "Leaving so early, Markie?" said one of them. He ignored the two men and walked out into the street.

Sidney

As he approached the stairway leading to the Department of Literacy Studies on the second floor, Sidney saw a shapely and long-legged young woman coming languorously down the steps. His eyes were so fixed on her, he missed his first step and fell. She laughed at him.

"Is your beauty caused it," he said.

"You men are always blaming woman for your fall," she said as she continued walking.

Sidney pulled himself up from the floor and gazed at the erotic movement of her hips as she walked down the corridor. She turned, looked at him and laughed again.

When, a few weeks later, he saw a mover's truck enter his apartment complex, and this said beauty came out of the cab and opened a door close to his own on the ground floor, he felt like singing praises to the gods that be.

She noticed him and said, "So it is you, The Stumbler!"

"You moving in here?"

"Yes."

"Would you like me to help you unpack?"

"Thanks, but my boyfriend is coming to help me."

A blue Toyota SUV drove in and parked. A handsome East Indian man in a white bushjacket came out and walked towards them.

"This is Dr Ganesh Behary, a cardiologist," said his new neighbour. "Please meet Mr..."

"Alexander, Sidney Alexander. And you are?'"

"Tammy East."

"Welcome to Golden Shower Manor," said Sidney. "It is named after that tree. I hope you will like it. If you need any help just call me, I am in No. 9." He went to his apartment.

After Tammy moved in, Ganesh became a frequent visitor, especially at night. Sidney soon recognized the sound of his car, and he would hear him driving out late or early morning.

One night, immediately after Ganesh left late, Sidney heard footsteps hurrying in the direction of his apartment, followed by an urgent knocking on his door. He got out of bed, pulled on a pair of shorts and opened the door. Tammy was standing there in her bathrobe. Without saying a word she pushed past him, tore off the bathrobe and got into his bed. He closed the door and joined her. She was still steaming with desire, and it was his wonderful opportunity to finish her off. Satisfied, she put on her bathrobe and left. They did not exchange a single word.

It was the start of a ritual between them. As soon as he heard Ganesh's car leave, he would hear Tammy's footsteps hurrying to his apartment. Ganesh seemed like a nice man so he felt a bit sorry for him in a 'there but for the grace of God goes I' kind of way. The falling of one was the rising of another. And he was certainly not going to complain about Tammy rushing into his bed. Then Ganesh stopped visiting. And one night, in the afterglow of their passionate and now even more intense exchange, and at the beginning of this new stage in their relationship, they had their first real conversation.

"What do you do?" asked Tammy.

"I am an assistant lecturer in literacy studies at the university where I fell at your feet. And I am also working on my PhD thesis."

"On what?"

"The history of literacy movements in Jamaica."

"That sounds very important."

"And what do you do?"

"I work in public relations, while working towards my masters in English. Our office is on the same floor as yours."

"Fate worked that one out very nicely."

"You are quite a lyrics-man aren't you?"

"Only when beautiful women bring it out of me. Let's celebrate with dinner soon. You like Chinese food?"

"Yes."

"There is that new one in the foothills called Bamboo Palace. I went there once. It has a very nice view of the city. Would you like to try it?"

"Sure."

They decided on a date and time.

At Sidney's request, the waiter took them to a table with a view of the city lights below. As they sat facing each other, Sidney continued feasting his eyes on the miracle that had just entered his relatively dry academic life. She wore her hair in a bun, and a light blue dress hugged her figure. Wooden earrings matched her necklace made from a similar material.

"My God! You are almost exceeding the beauty limit," he said.

She gave him that smile that Leonardo might have painted had he continued studying the physiology of women's smiles deep into his old age.

"You look nice in navy-blue," she said.

They both ordered the same red wine and toasted each other.

"To your thesis and the advancement of literacy!" said Tammy as they touched glasses.

"To us!" said Sidney.

Tammy ordered curried chicken and a salad. Sidney ordered the seafood hot-pot with bean curd.

"So why did you choose to study literacy?" asked Tammy.

"My father was virtually illiterate. Yet he loved words and was good at using them. He had a literary disposition and had he been literate he might have become a writer. I remember the moment with him when I made the decision to go into this field. There was a distance between us as I grew up. My mother was clearly on my side but I was very uncertain about him. He praised other children in the district very lavishly, in my hearing, but refused to compliment or encourage me even when, at my mother's suggestion, I told him I was coming first in my form. And my mother had to push him to help pay my school expenses. Then one year, while I was at high school, I won the literature prize and they gave me a copy of the complete works of William Shakespeare. I took the huge book home and my father saw me with it in the living room. It was the biggest book he had ever seen and he asked me what it was. Without explaining, I turned to my favourite play, Julius Caesar, and after a brief summary of the story up to that point, I read him the famous speech by Mark Antony. My father was thrilled. I had never seen him enjoy anything so much. I decided there and then that the advancement of literacy would be my thing. My decision to become a teacher of literacy was the first big choice of my life, and it has become my bedrock. I began reading Shakespeare to him from time to time. We started becoming friends and that would last for the rest of his life."

"The value of studying literature. Do you have siblings?"

"One brother that I barely knew. I should tell you that story. On one of my visits home, while both of my parents were still alive, as I was leaving the gate I saw an old woman in a red dress and black hat, and smoking a chalk-pipe, turning the corner, apparently on her way home from church, and as she saw me she said, 'When one of your parents die, that is when your brother and you going to come together.' It seems she was some kind of obeahwoman or warner-woman. And she was right.

"I started discovering that I had a brother, also the child of both of my parents, but who was raised by our grandparents. Neither my mother nor my father ever explained why this was so. Once when I mentioned him to my father he flew into a rage. My mother gave evasive answers to all my questions. Once or twice she urged me to get in touch with him, and I did manage to contact him, but a gap remained between us that I somehow never managed to cross. Nobody wanted to talk about him. He was a big mystery in my life. But whatever feelings they might have had about leaving their firstborn child with his grandparents, they seem to have taken them to the grave. It was their big silence. And I suppose that all of us must have our silences.

"Then when my father died, and I was in the throes of making the funeral arrangements, Mark showed up. We slept under the same roof for the first time on the night of our father's funeral, but he even refused to share a bed with me or my uncle who slept in my old room, and insisted on sleeping on the sofa in the living room. He returned to Kingston the following day, after promising to return to spend time with my mother. But he never did. He died three months later. And I buried him too."

The waiter brought the food and they began eating.

"The Chinese are amazing," said Tammy. "This curried chicken has that real old-time Jamaican taste like what my grandmother used to cook."

"I developed a taste for bean curd at a restaurant in England while I was doing my masters at the University of London. It is great with the fish and the lobster. And I love soy-sauce."

"So you were close to your father," said Tammy.

"Our connection got stronger and stronger over the years. When I visited home I sat for hours at the dining table listening to his stories. I drove him to the clinic. We were nearly the same size so I gave him some of my clothes and he loved wearing them. I read somewhere that a man has to stop being his mother's boy and become his father's son. That happened to me."

"And what about your mother?"

"I grew up being aware that there was a great tension between them. As a little boy I heard them quarrelling fiercely, with my father threatening violence, and my mother locking up herself in the bedroom to cry and pray. But I never found out what was the cause of this hostility. And I have no evidence that my father ever carried out any of his violent threats. My mother tried to get me to side with her against him but I refused. When I gave them money I divided it equally between them. I got a photographer to combine two of their photos into a single picture, and I got it framed and gave it to them as a wedding anniversary present. It hung in the living room for the rest of their lives. I still have it. But in spite of that tension they remained married for over fifty years. Not once did I see them express affection for each other. On his deathbed he praised me for doing so much for my mother, making her 'the luckiest woman in Mt Carlos', as he put it, and me for being 'a generous man', the only compliment he ever paid me openly. I almost cried at his funeral."

"And your mother?"

"I owe most of the good things in my life to her. It was she who worked hard at her dressmaking, craftwork and farming to send me to school. She left my decisions to me and rarely gave advice, but every time she did so it was rock-solid.

"After my father died a deep loneliness descended on her. She had grown up in a big family, and after those years with my father she found herself alone for the first time in her life. It took a heavy toll on her. After my father passed I noticed that she was seeing me with a different look in her eyes. I was the only close family member that she had left. It was now impossible to find suitable and reliable help in the district. I visited as often as I could. But she began developing dementia. This became dangerous when she began leaving the house and wandering away. It was a tough decision but I put her in a nursing home. She died there, after asking one of the nurses for me, I was told. Her funeral was in that same church to which she took flowers from her garden every Sunday morning. I refused her wish to be buried beside Mark, her firstborn. I buried her beside Lionel, remembering that bible verse that the way of a man and a maiden is among the things beyond the understanding of the wisest preacher.

"After my mother died they vandalized our home and stole all the contents and fixtures. Except for my books. Advocates for literacy will have a tough time in this country. On one of my visits there to look at the ruins, as soon as I was leaving the gate I saw the same old woman in the black hat and red dress, smoking a chalk-pipe, coming around the corner. I was frightened for I thought she was a duppy. But she was real enough. As soon as she saw me she said, 'The story of you and your brother is a twist on the parable of the Prodigal Son. This time it is the elder son who is the prodigal. But this prodigal never returned home. Neither the father nor the younger son was able to receive him into a home.' She stared into my eyes. 'You never hear about me? They call me Mama Truth.' She continued walking up the road humming to herself. I headed for my car a bit dazed.

"Seeing myself as the sole survivor of our small family, I began developing an interest in ancestry. I applied to the Registrar General's Department for my family tree. I found that my mother was a teenage mother when she had Mark. They got married three years later. Our father's name was not on Mark's birth certificate. All this shocked me. I had never for a moment imagined any of this. I am still struggling with this discovery."

"Thanks for sharing so much of your story with me. My father is a tomato farmer in St Elizabeth and my mother is a postmistress. I have four sisters and two brothers. But this dinner is for your story. I will tell you more about mine the next time we go out."

"Agreed."

"I saw photos of several women on the walls of your apartment," said Tammy with a mischievous grin.

"I will tell you about the main ones," said Sidney.

After the meal the waiter came and offered a choice of dessert. They agreed to share a serving of coffee ice-cream.

"What is your best memory of your parents?" asked Tammy.

"When I was a little boy, perhaps seven or eight, we had one of the heaviest rainfalls I can remember in all my life, next to one of the hurricanes. My mother said that the flying ants she noticed indicated that it might last for two weeks. And she was right. She was good at that kind of thing. We were locked in the house for days, surviving on shop-food like bread, bulla, biscuits, sardines, and canned and red-herring. We also ate ground provisions like yam, sweet potato, coco, dasheen, banana and plantain. My mother cooked on a charcoal stove she kept on the floor. She fried dumplings and fritters. She made coffee for my father and mint tea and cocoa for she and me. But we began running out of food.

"My mother told my father that he should use a crocus bag as a raincoat and go out on the farm to see if he could find anything to eat. He went out into the pouring rain. He returned with a big roasting breadfruit, the biggest one I could recall ever seeing. He said he saw it high up in a tree, and it was the only one he could see. It was as if it was there waiting for us. It was the first time he ever climbed a tree in the rain, but he managed to pick it.

"My mother roasted it, scraped the skin until it was crisp and brownish yellow. She opened it revealing its yellow heart. She cut it into slices and removed the inedible sections of each slice. We ate it with roasted saltfish. It was one of the greatest meals of my life."

Sidney looked into Tammy's dark-brown eyes and said, "If I ever meet a woman I can roast a breadfruit with like that, I will get married."

Tammy chuckled.

They both looked away.

Their eyes met again and locked.

They chuckled together for a longer time.

A Gift Of Yams

M*aas Bertie awoke at dawn, knowing that he* was about to repeat the ritual he had been performing every Christmas Eve morning for the past forty-three years. He would go to his field and dig the very first yam-hill that he planted each year, hoping it would bear an abundance of yams to be given as Christmas gifts to Uncle Mackie and his wife Aunt Esther, (affectionately known as Aunt Essie), whose generosity when he was a lost young man, had given him shelter and security, and the encouragement to go to the United States to be a farmworker, which had made it possible for him to buy the land and build the house in which he now lived. He could tell from his wife's breathing that she was still soundly asleep. He got up quietly so as not to wake her. Then he put on his drudging clothes, a worn khaki shirt and pants, and went outside to the yard and into the bathroom. He came out and walked to the kitchen door and went inside. He came out carrying a basket digging-bill, and a machete.

He crossed the yard and stopped in front of the hibiscus hedge which separated his home from his farm. He glanced up at the sky. The faithful Morning Star, his only companion during these yearly digging-and-giving, was still there, mounting higher and higher. He put the digging-bill and basket on the ground and began pruning the top of the hibiscus hedge. This ritual was one he performed each morning, before or after breakfast, but always before he left the house for work. The result was that the top of the hedge was as thick as a carpet.

He did not have the skill to sculpt it into the geometric forms, such as the blocks and spheres that he had seen on hedges around homes in the suburbs of Florida. This hedge was the least useful object on his property since it contributed nothing to the tangible prosperity of his household, and it did not put any money into his pocket. But pruning these shrubs that grew out of the land made him feel another kind of deep connection with it. He also felt that the care and beauty that it showed reminded him and visitors that this was a human habitation. The pruning completed, he slung the basket over his right arm and put the machete and digging-bill in it; then he walked past the house until he came to a path which led downhill into the eastern valley. He began whistling as he went down the path, sometimes walking and sometimes almost dragging himself, as the variation in the steep terrain required.

He got to the yam-field. The forest of yam-sticks, made mostly from bamboo, and covered with the weight of the yam-vines which had climbed up on them, leaned forward in unison towards the slope of the hill in front of them.

Their dark, shadowy forms seemed like a congregation of darkly-clad Muslims about to bend down in prayer. He stopped at the very first hill, the one at the extreme left of the front row of sticks. The withering of the vine suggested that it had completed its work in the air and sunlight, and that the fruits of its mysterious processes — he experienced a sense of awe at the wonders of nature manifested in the crops he cultivated — were waiting for him under the soil.

He put the basket and machete aside, and with an excitement well-known to farmers, and potters about to open a kiln after a firing, he began digging the yam-hill with the digging-bill. His digging was a collaboration between the digging-bill and his fingers, for he did not want the metal tool to damage the yams. He searched the yam-hill like an eager archaeologist hoping to find the treasured object he had good reason to believe was under there. But what if the yam-hill had been a failure and had borne nothing? He would simply move to the next yam-hill, and on and on until he found one good enough for the Christmas present. But like money that one earmarks to purchase a particular object, and which could not be substituted by putting it into the bank and then withdrawing it, similarly it would not feel right if the gift came from some other yam-hill than the one specifically planted for that purpose. Finally he felt a long, protruding object and his heart leapt. A yam! Excited, he began searching in the yam-hill furiously, but carefully, because he did not want to break the yam into pieces before he had seen it whole. At last, with the soil loosened all around, he pulled up the big yam triumphantly, with three big 'toes', their largest being nearly a foot in length, hanging from the resurrected 'head' that he had planted, and which he would retain to plant again for the following year's crop. "At least three of them can roast," he said as he used his machete to cut them from the head. He put them in his basket and began retracing his steps up the hillside.

Back in the bedroom he whispered to his half-awake wife that he would be taking the yams to Uncle Mackie and Aunt Essie. "Tell dem Merry Christmas for me," she said. She knew, understood, and appreciated the meaning of his ritual very well. "Breakfast will be ready when you come back," she said as she turned and sank her head into the pillow.

Maas Bertie returned to the bathroom, washed and put on some street-clothes for the walk to the McFarlanes. Like most of his countrymen, he believed that one should always look good in public, even if one is travelling a short distance. The daylight showed him more clearly as he began leaving his yard. He was a dark-skinned man of medium height, in his late sixties or early seventies, with very short hair and a receding hairline, and a long thoughtful face, and he wore a plaid shirt, blue jeans and black shoes. His dark, reflective eyes, and the prominence of his brow added depth to his look of being a thoughtful man, making him look like someone whose life had been a long hard struggle, but who also knew how to count blessings; and the gentleness around his mouth also suggested that he had the ability, much appreciated by those who knew him, to laugh heartily at life's ironies. In his right hand he carried a small navy-blue bag marked AIR JAMAICA, which contained the two yams he had carefully wrapped in an old newspaper.

He followed a path along the hillside, and finally got to the intersection where the road that came up from the eastern villages in the deep valley on his left, met the much bigger parochial road. After turning right onto this road, he began following it southwards. It was sandy, ochre-coloured soil, and the road was punctuated by man-made drains which, in all cases, swung from the gutter on the right, across the road, and down into the fields and bushes of the valley in the east. He could feel and hear his feet crushing the soft, grainy soil. It was all downhill, and the greater strain on his body for rhythmic motion, made his limp more noticeable, and one could see that there was something wrong with his left leg. He went as quickly as he could, in the rhythm of what seemed like a little pain-dance.

As he went down the road he remembered the story behind this annual gift of yams. His late mother, Miss Bertha London, was a helper in the household of Arthur Grayson, a coloured planter who owned a lot of land at Mt Carlos and the surrounding districts. While attending a dance in the district—some say it was her very first dance—she was 'fallen' by a sweet-talking stranger who had come to the district from God knows where, who left after the dance and his deed, and was never seen or heard of again. He, Bertrand London, was the offspring of that fall, and since his father's name was unknown, he had been given his mother's surname. Grayson was very fond of Bertha and adopted him. He had grown up as a member of Grayson's large family and, except for his dislike of the term 'the black son', sometimes given to him by outsiders, he had felt fortunate being even an adopted member of such a large and respected family.

He had gone to the elementary school with Grayson's children, and knew how to read and write. But he had difficulty deciding on a trade. So he helped on Grayson's farm and developed some skill in taking care of the horses. He was especially fond of the big black stallion named Emperor. Many people encouraged Grayson to enter this beautiful and powerful horse in one of the two races—Easter and Christmas—which were held on the racetrack, a long plateau above Mt Carlos. But Grayson refused, saying he did not believe in gambling; he said he had too much horse-sense, which he said he had seen defined in Comic Dictionary as the sense possessed by horses which prevented them from betting on people! He, Bertie, wished that Grayson would yield, for the idea of becoming a jockey was starting to appeal to him. What a glory it would be, and what a recommendation to the racing authorities, if he could ride Emperor and win a race with him!

At the same time he was falling in love with Selena, the headmaster's half-Indian daughter. He never thought such a flawless complexion was possible, that long curly hair could do such things to a man's imagination, and that the mere look from a girl's eyes could make him feel so nervous it was as if all his bones were melting. The headmaster and his family were staunch Baptists, and the annual baptism in the river was coming up. He felt certain that they would attend both the watchnight service the night before, and the baptism itself the following morning.

Grayson was not a frequent church-goer, but had forced his entire family into regular attendance at the Methodist church. And woe be unto anyone who missed a service! He was contemptuous of persons without a religious affiliation, 'Nonarians' he called them, and felt that such uneducated barbarians were not only capable of just about anything, they were certainly also destined for hell-fire. Yet as a result of some long family tradition—

it was rumoured that his family contributed money for the building of the Baptist church, which, it so happened was also very close to his own home—a firmer bond had developed between him and the Baptist parsons than had occurred between him and the Methodist ministers. It was a long tradition that the parson who occupied the Baptist pulpit, would have the honour of riding Grayson's best horse to the river for the baptism, and that after the ritual, he would have Sunday dinner with the Graysons. The parsons changed from time to time, but for Grayson, the loan of the favourite horse and the baptism dinner which followed, were engraved in stone. One year Bertie heard Mama Gray, Grayson's wife, discussing the dinner, and he observed that the entire household was being galvanized towards it.

But he, Bertie, had another idea. Why should the Rev. G. Alvin Stuart, the incumbent Baptist parson, be given the honour of riding Emperor to the baptism? He had never fed the horse a single blade of grass, groomed him, or taken him for his exercise. That designation 'Rev.' was all it took to make him the beneficiary of all this kowtowing. Bertie decided that he, Bertland Montgomery London —it riled him a bit that the Graysons had not given him their surname—would ride Emperor to the baptism and impress the daylights out of Selena! She would look at him with new eyes, actually see him, after she saw the dignity, skill and grace with which he could ride a big and powerful horse.

And he did in fact ride the horse to the baptism, much to the admiration and envy of many of the men and boys. But Selena was nowhere to be seen. He heard later that a bad cold had kept her away from all the activities associated with the baptism.

As a result, the Rev. G. Alvin Stuart was offered one of Grayson's mules as a substitute, but he rejected the offer, and so, instead of reveling in that extra grandeur and power that being on the back of a horse gives a human being, he decided to ride Shank's pony instead, and so he led his singing white-robed choir on foot, as he walked nearly a mile down to what seemed the most winding and treacherous of roads, to the river.

Bertland's cheek was too much for Grayson to bear. It had made him look, in the eyes of the community, like a man who did not honour his agreements; who was not the master of his household; who had no respect for deep traditions; and whose decision could be overturned by a mere 'stable boy' in his home. Mama Gray said she thought he was about to have a heart attack. Over the years of their long relationship, she had seen him in all kinds of moods, but this was the first time she had seen something resembling murder in his eyes. She felt glad she had opposed his desire to purchase a gun, for she felt sure that this was one occasion when he would have used it. Grayson personally packed all of Bertie's possessions in a cardboard box and put it at the front door. He waited patiently for the sound of Bertie's footsteps approaching, then he went to the door. "So you turn man on me, eh?" he yelled. "Well, two bulls cannot reign in one pen! There will be only one bull in this pen, and that will be me! So you are a man? Well, go display your manhood and build your own house. Get out of my home, I say!" And with that he kicked the box towards the adopted son who had broken his heart.

Bertie could still recall the anguished crying and pleading of his mother as she bent her stomach and begged for him. She promised Grayson that Bertie would never do such a thing again. She asked him to have mercy on a fatherless boy. But Grayson stood his ground.

Bertie decided that there was no point begging. He had gone against the old man's rules and had gotten what was coming to him. So he picked up the box and put it on his head. He walked out of the yard with no idea whatsoever of where he might go. He was halfway up the road when he remembered that Grayson's daughter Esther (Essie), the adopted sibling he felt closest to, had recently gotten married to his friend Mackie, Grayson's cattle manager, and that they lived about a mile away. He headed for their home.

When he turned up at their door, as they were about to start their Sunday dinner, they invited him to their table. Mackie was amused by his story and had a good laugh over it. "And you didn't even get the girl!" he chuckled. "What kind of a cowboy show is that? But it shows that you are a man of ambition. You came from humble beginnings, almost born in a manger, actually, but you wanted to ride the biggest, strongest and most beautiful horse ever bred in these parts. And like the knights of old you wanted to win the heart of a fair lady. What is wrong with that? Grayson should have admired you, and he should have congratulated himself for having adopted a son made of such stuff. And I suspect that deep down Grayson admired you a bit. After all he was a young man once, and I hear that Mama Gray was quite a beauty in her day, the kind of beauty that could have driven even Grayson to rashness. So don't worry about him. After what you did he was duty-bound to kick your backside. But he will cool down. I don't know him to be a man who holds grudges. A disciplinarian, certainly. But a man who holds things against you in his heart? Not the Grayson I have worked for all these years. You and him may yet have a drink and laugh at this some day. (Something like that did in fact happen, Bertie now recalled.) You can stay with us as long as you like. Fortunately I own the title to this piece of land. Not Grayson. Grayson cannot come here, pull you out, and thump you up. Welcome, my friend."

For years he slept on a cot in the McFarlanes' living room. He was there for the birth of their son Tal (short for Neftali, the name of a poet his mother saw in a school book). Mackie knew a politician and he helped him get a ticket to go the USA as a farmworker. Aunt Essie saved the money he sent back. When he returned, he was able to buy a piece of land from one of Grayson's daughters, one of his adopted sisters who was moving to Kingston to get married, and who had said she would never have sold that land to anyone else. Then with much help from Uncle Mackie, who was also a carpenter, he built the house in which he now lived. He got married, not to Selena, but to a plump little postmistress, and they had five children, one boy and four girls. They would all be coming home for Christmas starting that evening.

When he planted his first yam-field on his own land, he planted a hill for Mackie and Essie.

He arrived at the square. A bus was unloading passengers, very likely relatives of residents who were coming back to the district for the holidays. Someone called his name and he waved back, but he did not delay. He wanted to complete his morning's mission so he could then concentrate on Christmas plans for his own family. He turned left onto the main road.

Minutes later, he was at the gate of the McFarlanes, and also his gate during his own young manhood. The rising sun was now peeping over the top of the big mountain. He began the difficult and painful walk down the gradient—the most difficult part of the journey—down the steep path until he came to the larger house that the McFarlanes had built after the demolition of the older one into which they had welcomed him. He knew their routines, so there was no need for any formalities. He walked beside the house to the back, where, as he expected, he could now see Aunt Essie's back as she cooked breakfast in the outside kitchen. She had insisted over the years that food cooked over a woodfire tasted better than that cooked on a gas or electric stove. She had a gas stove in the kitchen, one given to her by her son Tal, but she used it only when it rained.

"Oi Essie! Merry Christmas!"

She turned to face him. She was a small, light skinned woman with kind, brown eyes, and greying hair sticking out of the side of her blue headtie. She was wearing a white apron.

"Bertie! You are as sure as the birds singing in the trees!"

"The hill bore three nice ones this year, my three gifts for Christmas," he said smiling as he took the yams from the bag and showed them to her. "You can roast one for Christmas breakfast tomorrow morning."

"Yes. And the others will go well with my green gungo peas and ham-bone soup. How is your family?"

"Everybody is fine. We are making a determined effort to have the entire family together for Christmas dinner tomorrow."

"And how is Pearly?"

"Good. She was still sleeping when I left the house. She is very tired. Christmas is the busiest time at the post office."

"I will get some breakfast for you."

Maas Bertie began climbing the steps to the dining room on his right. The sun was now above the mountain, and its light came across the deep valley which nourished rivers, fields and homes, crossed the roof of the kitchen and shone on the back of Maas Bertie's plaid shirt. He peered into the half-gloom and could see Uncle Mackie at the head of the table, with his son Tal on his right. Uncle Mackie, his light skin still deeply tanned by years of work in the sunshine, and in spite of his several years indoors as an invalid, was wearing a white vest and grey-blue pants. His unruly hair was in curls on top of his head; it lay down smooth and shiny only when he combed it. Tal, who sat in sideview on his left, was now a young man in his mid-twenties, and had his father's complexion and thick eyebrows, and his mother's thicker hair. He was wearing blue jeans and a white T-shirt.

"Oi! Merry Christmas!" said Maas Bertie as father and son looked up from their breakfast to greet him.

"Greetings, me dear sah," replied Uncle Mackie.

"Hi Papa Bertie," said Tal.

Maas Bertie laid out the newspaper wrapping on the floor beside the wall and placed the two yams on top of it. Then he sat on the floor in the doorway. "The hill bear better this year than last year: two nice pieces instead of one."

"We thank you very much," said Uncle Mackie. "I am going to ask Essie to roast one of them tomorrow morning. For me, on Christmas morning, nothing beats a nice piece of roast yellow-yam, scraped, with a piece of roasted saltfish, and a mug of strong, hot coffee. Dem can have all the ham and eggs in the world!"

"I will ask Mama to add a fried egg and a ripe banana or tangerine to mine," said Tal with a chuckle. "I love roast yam, too, but those will give it an additional buzz."

Aunt Essie came up the steps carrying a plate of ackee and saltfish cooked in coconut oil. He could smell the aroma, with slices of roast breadfruit carefully and lovingly scraped until they had thin, light-brown crusts, a slice of harddough duck-bread, and a mug of their homegrown coffee.

"Thank you very much," said Maas Bertie as he took the plate and mug and rested them on the floor near the yams. "I always love tasting your hand," he said, looking into Aunt Essie's eyes and smiling. He began eating with a fork.

"So Bertie, how you doin' man?" asked Uncle Mackie.

"Giving thanks. The Bible says giving thanks is the most joyful thing in the world. A so me say too. I have a pain in my knee, so I have to be limping. But Jesus bear more than that on the cross. I am getting away with only a pain in my knee."

"What the doctor say?"

"I am to go and do an x-ray. In the meantime he gave me some tablets to ease the pain."

"The tablets help?"

"Not much really."

"That is all the doctor dem do nowadays: spray you with a shower of tablets and hope that one will hit the spot. And most times all of dem miss. I prefer the old-time bottle medicine. You had to make monkey-face to drink it, but that was because it was good for you."

"And how is your arthritis?"

"That word is another word for…what do the teachers call it? Thank you, Tal. That word is a synonym for pain.

At least, hopefully, it is only pain for the rest of your life. Nothing could be worse than having arthritis in hell, on top of everything else there! Both my hands are swollen. After years of taking care of Grayson's cattle, building so many houses and erecting walls for the government, my two hands are so swollen I can barely feed myself. I am having difficulty holding the handle of a cup, and managing the knife and fork. I do a little better with soup and porridge."

"And you have sugar, too, right?"

"So dem say. And Essie is following doctors' orders and trying to feed me as if I am a rabbit or a guinea pig. But why did Massa God make mango, pineapple and ripe banana if he didn't intend for us to enjoy dem?"

"You are to enjoy them in your youth, when the evil days come not, and then fast, and watch and pray in your old age," said Tal, smiling.

"You heard dat, Bertie? And I spent good money on this boy's education!"

They all laughed.

"And when are you going back, Tal? You still teaching at that faraway school in Westmoreland?"

"Yes, I am still at the same school. I am going back down on Wednesday."

"I will bring something for you to take back."

"Thanks, Papa Bertie. You nah less than fix me up everytime I come."

"The children coming this evening, and I have plenty things to do today. So I have to go now. Blessings for the Christmas."

"Wishing better health for both of us in the New Year, Bertie. And thanks as always for your Christmas gifts. And all the best to you and your family," said Uncle Mackie.

"'Bye Papa Bertie," said Tal.

They watched as he picked up the used utensils, rose, and being careful with his sick leg, made his way down the steps. They heard his parting wishes and blessings with Aunt Essie. Then they heard the slow rhythm of his limping walk as he passed outside the dining room. The sounds diminished as he went up the hill.

"For many, many years, each Christmas Eve, he has brought us yams from a specially planted hill in his field," said Uncle Mackie.

"Why?"

For the first time Uncle Mackie told his son the story of this annual gift of yams.

"I love this story," said Tal after hearing this bit of his family history. "It is almost like a parable. I have been calling him 'Papa Bertie' all these years without knowing why. I was so used to seeing him there, it had never occurred to me to ask why he was there. To me he was just part of the world. I won't stop calling him that. He will always be 'Papa Bertie' to me."

Fenkeh - Fenkeh's Triumph

H*is main claim to fame, I gathered from the* discussion, was that on one occasion he asked Teacher Brown a question which Teacher Brown was unable to answer. This small victory over the revered pedagogue did much for his prestige in the community, particularly among the schoolchildren who heard about it, and among his drinking partners, most of whom displayed the typical drinker's regard for learning.

I met him at the door of the small grocery shop as he was on his way out and I was on my way in. He smiled broadly and bade me a very high spirited good evening, before he brushed hastily past and continued on his way. In the shop I discovered the reason for his high spirits. He had just been permanently employed as the postman for the area, in succession to Maas Bobby who had died a few weeks before. This success of his had revived interest in the quality of his brain, and the subject was being very lively discussed by the five men in the shop.

Long Toe, the orator of the group, was dominating the discussion. He leaned with his back against the counter and had a bottle of beer in one hand and a lighted cigarette in the other. His four companions sat on a long bench in front of him and were quietly hearing him out. Their faces were barely discernible in the faint light of the kerosene lamp.

"Teacher Brown," said Long Toe retelling the story, "Teacher Brown used to come down to de square every once in a while to do his business at the post office, and to talk to Maas Will our shopkeeper, who was his good friend.

"While in the shop 'im hear de man dem talkin' eena de bar, and 'im walk round and go een deh to tell dem how-de-do. Everybody glad to see Teacher, for 'im was a real jocular man.

"Devenin' Teacher! Devenin' Teacher!" say de whole a dem.

"Some a dem get up and take off dem hat. Dem offer Teacher a drink but 'im refuse, say 'im don't take strong liquor. Anyway 'im settle for a soft drink."

Long Toe sipped his beer, took a pull at the cigarette and continued:

"Dem start talk 'bout all sorts of things—church, school, farming, cost of living, everything. But most of the talk was 'bout school days, and all the old man dem start telling Teacher 'bout fe dem school days, an' how those days were much better than present days, and how harder the books were to read than those the children reading now."

"Dat is no dirt," interrupted Maas Henry. "Dat is a fact. For is pure Anansi story de pickni dem reading nowadays."

"True," said Long Toe impatiently. "Anyway," he continued, "de arguments went on and on. All this while... ha! Ha! Ha!... All this while Fenkeh-Fenkeh sat there with his glass in his hand, looking up eena Teacher face as if it is the very first time 'im seeing a teacher."

The five men chuckled.

"And all of a sudden," continued Long Toe, "all of a sudden Fenkeh-Fenkeh put up 'im hand and say, 'Teacher! Bet you I ask you a question that you cannot answer.'

"Teacher laugh. 'My good fellow,' im say, 'I have never told anyone that I know everything in the world.'

"But everybody quiet now wanting to hear what kind of question Fenkeh-Fenkeh going to ask the learned Teacher.

"Fenkeh-Fenkeh say,'Teacher, which verse in the Bible have in all the letters of the alphabet except the letter J?

"Teacher laugh. 'Well...actually... I've never tried to find out,' im say. 'Which is it?'

"Fenkeh-Fenkeh smile and look round pon everybody else to see if anybody know the answer. Not a soul know.

"'Maas Williams!' Fenkeh-Fenkeh call to the shopkeeper. 'Bring your Bible come lend we'.

"Maas Williams went for the Bible. When 'im bring it Fenkeh-Fenkeh say, 'Find Ezra chapter 7 verse 21'.

"Maas Williams find de passage and read it aloud so we all could hear. Him read it over and over and they find and check the letter dem, they count the letter dem one by one and find out that Fenkeh-Fenkeh was right.

One sinting! De man dem laugh and lick Fenkeh-Fenkeh on 'im back and say dem never believe that 'im could know a thing like that'.

"'Where you learned that, Fenkeh-Fenkeh?' asked Teacher.

"'Sunday School, Teacher', 'im say. 'Sunday School! One of the first things I learn as a little boy. I was bright at Sunday school. It was the big school dat give me trouble'."

The five men laughed heartily when Long Toe finished the story.

"Him 'ave a good memory," said Maas Henry.

"Yes," agreed Maas Wilkie. "A glad 'im get a nice job. A only hope 'im can keep it."

A deep silence descended on the small shop. I rattled my coin on the counter and the shopkeeper came. I bought a pack of cigarettes and decided to linger around a little bit.

"The faces of learning are always fascinating," I said to myself.

Miss Love And Mister Lovemore

If names are not correct, language will not be in accordance with the truth of things.

CONFUCIUS

*A**fter winding up my career as a professor of* English at a university in California, my wife and I were back in Jamaica trying to purchase a retirement home somewhere on the northcoast. We were staying with friends in Hope Pastures in Kingston. The next Sunday afternoon as I was going through the newspapers, I came upon the obituary of Mr Philip Lovemore late of Mt Carlos District. I read it and it stirred a memory of a story my mother had told me shortly before I left to study in the States.

I was born in Mt Carlos but had received most of my education in Kingston, because rightly or wrongly my parents believed that the schools there were better, and they arranged for me to board with relatives. I visited Mt Carlos mostly during the holidays.

After receiving my visa to study at the University of California, and now preparing to leave the island, I paid a farewell visit to my widowed mother who was not happy at my leaving, but who supported my decision since she was convinced that my educational opportunities and life chances would be better in the USA.

I was spending the weekend with her. She was in the kitchen cooking lunch and I was in the living room sitting and reading. She called me to do something for her, and it turned out that she wanted me to open a tight jar. This was reminiscent of my holidays there. Like many Jamaican mothers she did not want her son spending too much time in the kitchen and becoming a 'maama-man', the local nickname for a man who did women's work. So she would call me to the kitchen only to do manly things like chopping wood, breaking coconuts and opening tight bottles and jars. I opened the jar and sat at the kitchen table since it would be an opportunity to talk to her some more; it would be a long time before we had a chance to converse again—it would be costly to fly to and from California.

"Last night I dreamt about Miss Love and Mister Lovemore," she said.

"Who are they?"

"You mean you don't know about the most famous love story to come out of this district? At least as far as I know. I bet you know about Antony and Cleopatra, Romeo and Juliet, and Napoleon and Josephine. But you don't know about Miss Love and Mister Lovemore."

"Lovemore. I vaguely remember the name. He was the headmaster of the elementary school, right?"

"Yes. And it was quite a story about him and his wife."

"It is an intriguing name and I love studying about names. So tell me about him."

I now remembered the gist of the story.

Miss Rita Love, a new graduate of Shortwood College came to the school first. She was the early childhood specialist and taught the lowest A&B classes. She was a young and shapely brown woman with an upturned nose, bright eyes and a very sunny disposition and a smile that made men glad to be alive. Her pupils loved her. The headmaster, Mr R. Stanley Grant, a much admired giant of an educator, literally and figuratively, had gone to the college to personally recruit her. A big cricket fan, he had introduced her to the school as his batting partner at the other end of the wicket: she would start the students off, and he as the teacher of the sixth and final class would give them the finishing touches. Long before female cricket, she loved to joke about the metaphor of her as a batswoman.

Two years later: enter Mr Philip Lovemore, recruited by Teacher Grant from Mico College, the men's college for teachers. He was of black complexion and always immaculately groomed with his white or blue shirts and neckties that matched his pants. His black shoes were so well polished people joked that you could see your face in them. He had a slow, relaxed walk with his head held back in a gesture of pride and self-assurance. He was assigned to the fifth class, right beside that of R. Stanley Grant, his mentor and recruiter. He taught all subjects but my mother remembered that he had a special love for poetry and mathematics. From his desk he could look down the passage on his left and see Miss Love sitting at hers.

The synchronization of their names—both names were also new to the community—was quickly noticed, and before long would-be matchmakers saw it as a divine gift to them. The two young teachers were at first surprised and amused by it. Before long it became a game between them. Philip would greet his colleague with a "Hello, Love." And she would reply, "Hello Lovemore." A mutual attraction may well have been at play from the very start, but the possible dynamic of their names must certainly have fanned the flame.

It was at this point, my mother said, that she entered the story.

She was in Mister Lovemore's class. One afternoon he called her to his desk and gave her a folded note to take to Miss Love. She made her way through the blocks of classes, feeling a bit like a goldfish in a bowl, as the eyes of the school watched her take this missive from Lovemore to Love. After reading the message Miss Love blushed and smiled to herself, and then added some remarks of her own at the bottom of the note and handed it to her to be returned to Mister Lovemore. So it was that my mother became the postwoman of their affair. The school got used to seeing her going back and forth carrying these notes. Soon the tongues of the other teachers began wagging, and the pupils began to suspect that something of an adult significance was going on between these two.

Both teachers stayed at the same boarding house in the district, and the owner had strategically assigned them to rooms at the opposite ends of the big wooden house. One Saturday evening my mother was sent to the house on an errand and she saw Mister Lovemore and Miss Love sitting in the shade of the mango tree in the yard. They seemed to be discussing poetry for she heard words like 'feet' and 'metre' coming from them, terms that Mister Lovemore had introduced them to in his class. She went over and greeted them, and they encouraged her to study hard. She completed her errand and returned home.

These two new teachers were eager to make their mark on the school. One Friday morning Mister Lovemore showed up at school wearing his scouting uniform. It sent a current of excitement through the boys, most of whom quickly joined the troop he formed, which was the first in that part of the island. Miss Love quickly followed by forming a Girl's Guide troop. Mister Lovemore formed a choral group to read poetry. Miss Love formed a choir.

Their poetic and musical interests soon bore fruit. Mister Lovemore played the guitar and loved composing his own songs, something a bit unusual at that time. Miss Love wrote her own poems, also an unusual pastime. Mister Lovemore set one of her poems to music and, introducing themselves as The Love and Lovemore Duo, they performed it at the next school concert. It was the biggest hit of the night.

Their song became the talk of the community and word began to spread beyond it. After another performance at the school, headlined by them, and put on to raise funds to repair the schoool's piano, their reputation made another big leap. After contributing to a concert at the church, they began receiving invitations to perform at other schools and churches in the parish. With their real, romantic names, and fresh-sounding delightful music which fused mento, merengue and gospel, they seemed destined for success.

Partly in order to please their mostly religious audiences, and partly as a result of Mister Lovemore's personal poetic interest in the Song of Solomon, his favourite book in the Bible, they decided to base their compositions on this biblical work. They wrote and sang songs with titles such as "Better than Wine", "Loving You with my Soul", "Eyes of a Dove", "Yuh Fair me tell yuh, yuh Fair", "You have Ravished my Heart", "My Bowels can tell me when you are Near", "Hair like a Flock of Goats", "Fruits of the Valley", "Love is as Strong as Death" and "Many Waters cannot Quench Love". My mother remembered many of these titles. And I collected others from asking persons who remembered the Lovemores. Had the Jamaican recording industry gotten off the ground by then, they may have become one of the famous male-female duos that arose during the early years of the music industry on the island.

Of course, they alone knew what they saw in each other, for they seldom spoke to others about their relationship.

It was no surprise when they announced that they intended to get married. The wedding was held at the Baptist church where Mrs Lovemore was an active member (Mr Lovemore was a Methodist). Boys from Mr Lovemore's scout troop and girls from Mrs Lovemore's Girl Guides formed a guard of honour for them as they left the church. My mother was one of the Guides. The reception was held in a booth in the yard of the boarding house where they stayed. Teacher Grant was the master of ceremonies, and he celebrated his role as the godfather of this marriage. Many colourful toasts played on the poetry of their names. At one point, Teacher Grant had to declare a moratorium on ribald allusions to their names in the toasts. The newlyweds sang one of their songs: "Many Waters cannot Quench Love". Then they had their first dance as man and wife to the music of a hired mento band. There was an abundance of food and drink, and it was a joyous day at Mt Carlos.

Then the couple announced an unusual thing. It was customary that teachers who came to that school, often right after graduation from college, served for a time and then they left. But the Lovemores announced that they intended to settle at Mt Carlos. They bought a piece of land, and with the help of local carpenters built their own home.

When they expected their first child there was much interest in what name they would give their offspring: Love+ Lovemore + ? Members of the community offered some very creative suggestions. But the Lovemores decided that they did not wish to saddle their children with unusual names, so they opted for Love + Lovemore = ordinary Jamaican names. Their first child, a son, was named Ian and the daughter who followed, Sharon.

When my mother's story ended, Mr Lovemore was now headmaster of the school, and Mrs Lovemore was his much-loved, motherly, and veteran batting partner at the other end of the wicket. Together they had put a lot of runs on the board.

I hadn't thought much about the couple until I saw Mr Lovemore's obituary in the newspaper. I rolled over on the bed, pointed it out to my wife Marilyn who was from another part of the island, and told her what I remembered about the story.

"That is a romantic story, What a pity your name is Ezra Wilkinson and mine is Marilyn Wolfe," she quipped.

The following day, while we were window shopping in one of the malls, we ran into Lloyd Mason, a former playmate of mine during my holidays at Mt Carlos: we had fished in the rivers, climbed coconut trees and picked fruits, and 'ran boats' by roasting dasheens on a woodfire beside the river.

"Oi Wilkie!" he hailed me as we met.

"Lloydie!" I replied.

We embraced and examined our changed but still recognizable selves.

"I read about Mr Lovemore's passing," I said.

A cloud passed over Lloyd's face.

"Mi sorry so till," he said. "That man taught me nearly everything I know about schooling. I am a contractor, and it is his mathematics and English I use every day. In his sixth class he used to call me up to his desk to read and calculate. He wouldn't leave it to any other teacher. He made sure to do it himself. And furthermore, he was like a father to me. I knew little or nothing about my real father. I was a member of his scout troop and we once hiked to Blue Mountain Peak. And Mrs Lovemore was like another mother to me. My parents used to give me produce from our farm to take to their cottage on Saturday mornings."

"Are you going to his funeral?"

"Me must be dere. You going?"

I turned to Marilyn and she nodded.

"See you there," I said.

On the afternoon of the funeral we drove in our rented car up to Mt Carlos. It felt strange going there now. My parents had passed away. My siblings and I had sold the property. With the exception of a few distant cousins, I had no more connections with the place.

Trying to be punctual, an American habit we had acquired, we left early intending to be there at least half-an-hour before the scheduled start of the ceremony. But we found the Baptist church, the same one in which the Lovemore's had got married— almost full. We managed to find seats near the back.

At the start of the service the preacher, a rotund black man with a powerful voice, announced with regret that Mrs Lovemore was ill and unable to attend the funeral. As the service progressed I recognized some of the familiar funeral hymns and scripture readings. It was interrupted when a screaming woman in white ran up the aisle to the preacher and whispered something in his ear. He announced to the mourners that Mrs Lovemore had passed away. The memory of what followed I shall take to my own grave. That sound of people weeping and wailing. And singing with a fervency I could not recall ever hearing in a church before. Ian and Sharon, teachers and students from the school, church leaders, members of the community, and a politician half-spoke and half-wept through the tributes. The choir sang one of their best-loved songs, "Fruits of the Valley". Mr Lovemore's funeral became partly that of his wife's.

The preacher announced that the same hearse that had brought Mr Lovemore's body from the funeral home to the church, and that was waiting outside to take it to the burial plot there at Mt Carlos, would take that of Mrs Lovemore's back to the same home.

It was in a charged emotional silence that Marilyn and I drove back to the city.

I was unable to attend Mrs Lovemore's funeral since I was contracted to teach a summer course at my university and had to leave to the island shortly after.

When I returned, I called Lloyd Mason to ask how it went.

"Wilkie, it is hard to separate those two funerals in my mind," he said. "Part of Mr Lovemore's was also Mrs Lovemore's, and part of Mrs Lovemore's was also Mr Lovemore's. Things about the two personalities came out, like —Mr Lovemore's gifts as a teacher, and Mrs Lovemore's work in the church and the community. They were buried pretty much as they lived."

"You needn't say anymore, Lloydie," I said.

Reflecting on them now, it seems as if they lived up to the Confucian view of the link between names and truth. I also recall Saul Kripke's view that names are 'rigid designators', true in all possible worlds, presumably including in an afterworld if there is one.

Love's Last Messenger

Mr Fisher, the headmaster of the new secondary school, looked up from his desk and saw Miss Sandra Singh, the new social studies teacher, standing and smiling at the door of his office.

"Come in, Sandra," he said. He called her by her first name because he felt a certain intimacy with her, as a result of the relationship he had had with her sister Helen some twenty-five years before. At the time Sandra had been a pretty little girl in first form. He was pleased that the Chairman of the Board of Governors had offered Sandra a job at the school; it was like having a part of Helen with him.

Sandra entered the office and sat in the chair which Mr Fisher offered her. She was now a plump young lady and beginning to look like her mother, as Mr Fisher remembered her. Sandra smiled at him and Mr Fisher noticed her even, attractive teeth which resembled Helen's.

"Helen sends hello for you," said Sandra.

"It is very nice hearing from her. I haven't had news of her for a long time. Is she still at that school in... St Ann was it?"

"Yes, but she isn't at school now. She is at home. She isn't well."

"Oh?"

"She has cancer."

"Cancer! That could be serious."

"It is. She is getting treatment. But I might as well tell you. The doctors are not very optimistic."

"Oh my God!" said Mr Fisher as he rested his elbows on his desk and put his face in his hands for a moment.

"But she is cheerful," said Sandra. "She is determined to fight it. She is talking about going back to school one day."

"Please give her my very best wishes. Give me her address so I can write to her."

He gave Sandra a piece of paper and she wrote the address and a telephone number on it and returned it to him.

"I know she will be happy to hear from you," said Sandra in a manner which suggested that she knew a good deal about the relationship between Helen and Mr Fisher. Then, explaining that she had a class coming up, she left the office.

Mr Fisher sank into reverie and remembered the very first time he had seen Helen. He was sitting in a bus in the parking lot of the Westmoreland Senior School and listening to the throttle of the engine as he waited for the bus to drive off and begin the long journey back to Mount Carlos in the eastern section of the island. He was in his final year of high school, and he was a member of a group of students who had just completed a week-long educational tour of the nearby sugar estate. The trip was a gift to his school by the general manager of the estate who had been impressed by the school's performance in a national agricultural competition. Now, after the stimulation of the talks and the sights, the pleasure of camping at the sports club, and the novelty of seeing so many persons of Indian descent, the unfamiliar plains and the miles of canefields, and of seeing so many people riding bicycles and motorcycles, he was about to return to his very different home in the hills.

He turned to look at a group of schoolgirls in their green and white uniforms who were conversing in one of the buildings near to him. One of them, an Indian girl, had such a lovely profile it made him feel a sweet, exquisite warmth in his heart, and when she turned and he saw the full beauty of her face and figure, it made him gasp. She was listening to her friends who seemed to be trying to persuade her to accept some view; she listened with a gracious placidity and smiled when they raised their voices insistently. He felt the bus move forward. The girl and her friends glanced at the departing bus without much interest, but even that brief look in his direction gave him a better view of her large and lovely eyes. The girls returned to their conversation before the bus was out of sight. He continued thinking of her as they drove away, and his memory of her, especially her eyes, remained his most enduring memory of his week's visit to the sugar estate.

The night after hearing about Helen's illness, Mr Fisher dialed her number. He was excited by the prospect of hearing her voice again after so many years. Perhaps her husband would answer the phone; Mr Fisher had never met him, but he knew that Helen married him shortly after the breakup of their relationship. He got a busy signal. He waited and tried again but the busy signal persisted. After several more attempts, that night and the following night, he concluded that the phone was out of order. He decided to write to her instead.

After school the following day, he went to a pharmacy in the nearby town to buy a greeting card. The funny ones seemed too frivolous, and the optimistic ones wishing a speedy recovery struck him as being vainly inappropriate. He noticed that there were no cards for the terminally ill. He bought a card without words, and when he got home he wrote in it to Helen, telling her that he was thinking of her, and that his greatest wish for her was that she would not suffer very much. He mailed the card the following day.

One afternoon a few weeks later, Sandra arrived at Mr Fisher's office carrying a stuffed envelope. "Helen was very happy to hear from you," she said, "and she sends some photographs to show you." Sandra stood on Mr Fisher's left and explained each picture as she put it on the desk in front of him.

There were pictures of Helen's two daughters, one in her late teens and the other in her early twenties. One wanted to go to university, the other was a teller in a bank. They were attractive young women, and Mr Fisher could see Helen's beauty in their features. But there was also an African presence in their fuller lips and thicker hair; these young women were clearly Afro-Indians, or Douglas as they are called in Trinidad and Guyana. He thought of how close he had come to being their father. What would they have looked like had they been his children? There would have been a bit of Europe in them as well, he thought. When he and Helen were dating, people had often commented on what beautiful children they would have; people seemed to like the brown/Indian combination. But that had not happened.

"They are very interested in meeting you," said Sandra. "They know a lot about you."

"Really!"

"Everyone who knows Helen knows about you," said Sandra. "She never stopped talking about you."

Then she showed him a recent photo of Helen lying on a bed. She had put on quite a bit of weight, but still had much of the stunning figure that he remembered. Her hair was now cut short, and looked like an Indian/Afro. During their years together she had worn it hanging down, the way he told her he liked it. Perhaps her dark-skinned husband preferred the Afro-look, he thought. After he remarked on the new hairstyle Sandra said, "It is the result of the chemotherapy. It made her lose her hair, but it is now growing back."

"She doesn't look ill," said Mr Fisher.

"If you didn't know you could never tell," said Sandra.

He recalled that Helen had been remarkably healthy in her younger years; she told him once that she had never been to a doctor. He recalled the saying, "Plenty sick, long life; little sick, short life."

"Tell her thanks for introducing me to her beautiful daughters," he said as Sandra returned the pictures to the envelope. "I hope to meet them someday. They will keep reminding me of her."

After Sandra left, Mr Fisher recalled the beginning of his relationship with Helen.

The year after seeing her for the first time on the school outing, and being smitten to the bones by the experience, he had entered Mico College to be trained as a teacher. He had specialized in English and Visual Arts, but had no career plans whatsoever. One of the lecturers loved the paintings he had exhibited as part of his course-work, and offered to recommend him for a job at the Westmoreland Senior School where her brother-in-law was the headmaster. Their art room had been closed for years, she said, because they could not find a suitable teacher. She was convinced he was the man for the job. But the very first thing that the name of the school had conjured up in his mind was the picture of the beautiful Indian girl with the soulful eyes, and the profile that had made his heart sing. "I would love to apply for the job," he said at once. He set the formalities in motion immediately, and a few weeks later he was offered the job by the Chairman of the Board. Fate had showed him the beautiful girl, and something like fate had given him a job at the school where he had seen her for the first time. But would fate lead him to her a second time? He told himself that if it did, it would surely be a sign that fate was trying to tell him something important.

A few months after he started working at the school he saw her again. The exact moment came back to him vividly. It was after school and the evening classes were in session. He had stayed behind to talk with one of the senior teachers who had taken a motherly interest in him (he was only twenty years old, and at the time this was very unusual for a graduate of a teachers' college); his mentor was sitting at her desk in her classroom and he was standing at the door on the corridor. He turned and saw an attractive young Indian woman walking gracefully down the driveway on the other side of the lawn. He recognized her at once and asked the senior teacher who she was. The teacher told him her name was Helen Singh, and that she was a past student of the school, and was now working as a pre-trained teacher at a nearby primary school. She visited the school often to see her brother who was on the staff, and her younger brothers and sisters who were students. Pleased that the gods seemed to be on his side, he resolved to make her acquaintance at the earliest time possible.

He started a conversation with her the next time he saw her in the netball playing area, while they were waiting for a match to begin. His opening line was: "Good evening, Miss Singh. I have been carrying a picture of you in my head for the past four years! And now here you are!"

Her eyes shone and she gave him the same warm, gracious smile that he had not forgotten. She said she had been hearing a good deal about the new art teacher.

In that first talk he discovered that she wanted to go to college to be trained as a teacher, and was curious to hear about college life from a recent graduate, like him. She came to his classroom after school one evening, and they sat and talked for hours. She began visiting him there often. He remembered the evening when she sat looking at the floor, not wanting to look at him and show the feeling in her eyes, and he felt the thick, erotic telepathy between them. They began taking walks together, and he would sometimes push her bicycle for her. There was the unforgettable first kiss as he walked her home one night after a movie, the exciting sensation of the lips of a real woman moving beneath his, for the first time in his life. There were the love poems he wrote to her. And there were the times when she sent one of her brothers to the home where he boarded, to tow him to her home on his bicycle, and to travel for miles in nights scented with the sweet aroma of ripe sugar cane being processed at the factory. The bell sounded, reminding Mr Fisher of his responsibility for the school.

The next time Sandra visited his office she wasn't smiling. Strain was showing in her eyes. When she sat she bent forward, unable to relax. But there was a motherly maturity in her voice when she said: "We are rushing Helen to New York for treatment. Her doctor recommends it."

"Do you have any relatives over there?"

"She is going to stay with her husband's sister in the Bronx."

"It is a good thing she has a supportive family. I wish there was something I could do."

"It means a lot to Helen to know that you are thinking of her now, and that you are on her side."

Mr Fisher had difficulty falling asleep that night. The story of his affair with Helen kept running through his mind. He tossed and turned as he thought about it.

He had done well at the school that first year, and was offered a scholarship to Canada to do further studies in the visual arts. It brought about a crisis in their young relationship. It was scheduled to be a four-year scholarship, and both doubted that their young affair could stand such a strain. But after arriving in Canada he discovered that the programme of studies would lead to a diploma and not a degree, and he felt that in his credentials-obsessed country; this might not be sufficiently recognized. The scholarship authorities in Canada said they would transfer him to a degree programme only if the Jamaican Ministry of Education requested this. But in spite of all his efforts and theirs, they failed to get a reply of any sort from the ministry. He decided to return to the island and pursue degree studies elsewhere.

In the meantime Helen had achieved her ambition and was now a student at the St Joseph's Teachers' College in Kingston. They kept up a lively correspondence between Canada and Kingston. Helen sent him a studio photograph of herself in a figure-hugging dress standing beside a huge Grecian vase; he thought the two symmetries complemented each other wonderfully. She had her dark, beautiful hair hanging down to her shoulders, and as always, there was the warm, gracious, benevolent smile. His Canadian landlady noticed the photo on the wall of the basement room in which he lived, and often teased him about it. "All my boys have found lovely mates, and I hope you will one day too, Lloyd," she kept saying.

When he returned to Jamaica he got a job in Kingston so he could be close to Helen. They went to movies and dinners and parties at her college; they took bus trips to the outskirts of the city. His flat was their cosy retreat where they spent happy times by themselves.

He was an attractive young man, one woman told him, who, much to her approval, didn't behave as if he knew he was attractive. There were other girls whom he noticed and dated from time to time. But everyone who knew him knew that Helen was the special one. One of his closest friends — a notorious womanizer — recognized the tenderness of his feelings for Helen, and once remarked that that was how a man ought to feel about his wife, and that he himself would get married if he ever felt that way about a woman.

Mr Fisher tried to get at what he thought was the heart of Helen's feelings by recalling her most memorable expressions of endearment. He remembered the concern and affection in her voice when, on one of the occasions when he was to be towed home, she cautioned her brother not to let him fall from the bicycle; they had all laughed, but he remembered the real emotion in her voice; she did not want him to get hurt in a bicycle accident. Once, while caressing her hair, he asked her why she liked him, "Because you are lovable," she said without hesitation. It wasn't great poetry, but it was the first time he had heard a woman use a word rooted in 'love' to describe him. Most of all there was the same inscription she wrote on the back of all the photographs she sent him "To Lloyd – From Helen, your true love."

"Women, women, in my life," said Mr Fisher to himself as he tossed in his bed, "which of you has loved me most of all?" Helen, something in him answered. She was gentle, and he sensed in her, the depth of the proverbial quiet river.

The breakup came when he decided to go back overseas to do further studies. He had left the high school to join the staff of a new teachers' college being founded in Mandeville. But for him this was only a step in the direction of further education. He had come to the conclusion that he was a better academic than an artist, and so would return to the field of English studies. He decided that he wanted to achieve the highest possible qualifications. He felt he was too young for marriage. He would wait. Breaking up with Helen was painful, for in addition to his appreciation of her stunning beauty, he also had very warm, tender and caring feelings for her. She was still at her college in Kingston and he saw her less frequently. Furthermore, when he saw the many pretty young women at the college, most of them near his own age, he felt it would be unwise to get married and settle down, which was what Helen wanted to happen right after her graduation. So he wrote Helen a letter ending their affair. She wrote a grief-stricken reply to what she called his "heart-rending" letter. But she also commended him for the manner in which he had brought the affair to an end.

When Sandra appeared at the door of his office a few days later, he could tell from her expression that she was the bearer of sad news.

"Helen has passed on," she said after she sat down.

Mr Fisher knitted his brow and stared at the papers on his desk. His first serious girlfriend had died and he felt diminished: Helen's side of what they had created together was now mostly gone. The death of a first girlfriend was not a milestone he had ever thought of before. There had been a number of recent deaths in his own family, and he felt he had moved over to the death-half of his life's continuum.

Sandra said, "She died at home in the arms of one of her daughters."

"Helen was very special to me," said Mr Fisher, finally letting Sandra see some of his emotion.

"I know," said Sandra, her dark-brown eyes shimmering with understandings she did not put into words. Mr Fisher saw her as a timely and chance emissary from his past, reconnecting him with Helen in her final days. He felt that Sandra knew a good deal about Helen's feelings for him, and that she was getting some satisfaction from her role as love's last messenger.

Sandra said, "The funeral will be next Saturday at St Margaret's at three o' clock."

"I will try to be there," said Mr Fisher.

After supper that evening, he felt like talking to someone about Helen, and he decided to tell his household helper about her. He opened a drawer and took out the envelope in which he kept photographs of his former girlfriends, and after thumbing through pictures of Carol, Lydia, Carmen, Bernice, Gloria and Lois he came to 'The Beauty beside the Grecian Vase'. A flood of recollections filled his mind as he looked at the picture, his eyes moving over the form he once knew so well. He went into the living room and sat and waited for the helper to come out of the kitchen.

"Have a seat Miss Alice," he said when the helper appeared at the door, "I have something to show you."

Miss Alice sat in the easy chair facing him. She was slim and dark complexioned and was wearing her usual head-tie. She had often showed a discreet curiosity about his love life, and her eyes lit up when Mr Fisher handed her the photograph. As she studied the picture, he told her the story of his affair with Helen.

"She is a very pretty young lady, sar," said Miss Alice. "How come you let her drop outa your hand? Me sorry fe hear about the death." Mr Fisher took the photograph.

Miss Alice continued: "And you mustn't think that it was a good thing you didn't marry her, since she would have left you a widower so soon."

"Such a thought never occurred to me," said Mr Fisher.

"You just remember the nice memories," advised Miss Alice.

On the day of the funeral, Mr Fisher stood at a window at home and watched the rain pouring down. His car had holes in the floor and he had fears of flooding on the plains. The headlights of his car were also poor, and he had doubts about a long night's journey on a wet, unfamiliar road. But was he merely rationalizing? he asked himself.

Perhaps the real flood he feared were the emotions likely to be released in him by meeting her husband, children and the relatives he knew in those early years. Everyone saw him then as Helen's young man.

As he watched the streaks of water on the glass he remembered the last time he saw Helen. It was at Sandra's graduation dance, and he had gone there with the woman he was then dating, thinking of it only as another dance to go to. But he met Sandra on the dance floor and she told him what the occasion was, and that Helen and other members of their family were sitting in the southeast corner of the auditorium. He and his date sat out the next dance and he asked to be excused and went in search of Helen. He found her sitting quietly, looking beautiful and mysterious in the dark. She seemed very pleased to see him. He bent over and kissed her on the left cheek. The music was too loud for conversation, so after standing there for a few minutes, he squeezed her hand, asked to be excused and went back to his date.

That was how he wanted to remember her, he thought, looking reflectively at the rain. He decided not to go to the funeral. He wanted his last memory of seeing her to be that final kiss on her left cheek.

Sandra brought him a report on the funeral a few days later.

"I thought you were coming to the funeral," she said, showing her disappointment: the story had not ended the way she wanted it to.

Mr Fisher described how bad the weather was.

Sandra continued: "She was buried in a vault in the yard of the home she and her husband finally built; but they never lived in it, not even for a day."

Mr Fisher listened as she recounted details of the funeral: the packed church in spite of the rain; the performance by children from Helen's former school; the abundance of cars as well as some trucks and buses.

Mr Fisher handed Sandra a piece of paper. "I would like to write to her mother. Please give me her address." Sandra wrote on the paper and returned it.

Then she took a plastic card from her handbag and handed it to Mr Fisher. On one side was a picture of Jesus as the Good Shepherd carrying a sheep, and with Helen's full married name printed at the bottom; on the other side were the words of the Twenty-Third Psalm.

"Thanks for the souvenir," said Mr Fisher.

As he watched Sandra leave, he felt a warm affection for her rise inside him; she was now like a relative, and would be an ongoing link with his memories of Helen. Of course, he thought, Sandra had come to his school for a job, but had no idea of the story that had brought him there, that had made it possible for him to receive the message of love that she had brought to him from Helen.

After breaking up with Helen, he had broken up with Carol in the USA over his decision to return to the island. And he had broken up with Lydia in Jamaica over his decision to return to the States to do his master's degree in education. And he had broken up with Carmen in the USA, when he decided to return to the island to settle down and teach. Unable to get a good job as a headmaster on the island, he had finally decided to migrate to the USA to find a job there. Bernice did not want to accompany him to the USA or to wait in Jamaica for him to find a job there, so he had broken up with her in Jamaica.

But finding a job in the USA had proven very difficult. He had knocked about for months without any success.

Then he saw an advertisement that representatives from the Jamaican Ministry of Education were at a hotel recruiting teachers for schools in Jamaica. He went there, made an application and was invited to an interview. The result was that he was offered a lucrative post as principal of one of the finest new secondary schools on the island. Perks included return airfare, a cottage on the campus, an entertainment allowance, and tax benefits. He accepted the post with much glee, and a sense of irony that made him laugh aloud after he read the job offer. He thanked the Americans for the visa to a job in his own country, as a 'foreign expert!'.

And one day Sandra Singh, a woman from his past, had entered his office with one of the most fundamental and important stories of his life.

After she left he picked up the souvenir card and looked at it carefully again. He read The Twenty-Third Psalm for the first time in many years. Then he read it again, looking for a sentence or phrase he could hold on to. His eyes settled and lingered on the words: "He restoreth my soul."

That night as he lay in bed, he found himself thinking about the various women in his life. Since returning to the island he had had affairs with Gloria and Lois. He had broken up with Gloria because she was very anxious to have a baby, but the baby seemed more important to her than he was to her; he felt she saw him primarily as the means to the baby and its future. It was flattering to be in such demand, but he wanted a woman who loved him for himself, first. Then he would get around to talking about babies. He was still dating Lois.

It seemed to him that he had had a good reason for every breakup, but most people would probably find so many breakups abnormal. Except perhaps someone like Cassanova, for whom every relationship must lead to a breakup, so that the door to a new conquest can be opened. But he did not think of himself as a Cassanova. Could it be that underneath all those reasonable sounding breakups there was some unconscious explanation that he was unaware of? Should he get himself psychoanalyzed?

Could it be that he had what he once called The Sinbad Complex? As a boy he had read of an Arabian sailor named Sinbad who was shipwrecked on a deserted island covered with precious stones. He began picking them up and stuffing them into his pocket. But he kept seeing bigger and more beautiful ones ahead of him. So he would throw away the ones he had and go after the more attractive ones. He couldn't remember the end of the Sinbad story. But could it be that he was driven by an insatiable lust for women the way Sinbad was driven by his lust for jewels? Such stories seldom have happy endings, he thought. Would his pursuit of the gems of higher education also lead to some unsatisfactory Sinbad-like ending? Perhaps that was the point of Helen's message.

He picked up the phone and dialed Lois's number. As soon as he heard her answer he said:

"How is my lady with skin as dark and beautiful as the night?"

He heard her laugh, and then she said, "As soon as I heard the phone ring I thought it might be you."

"Telepathy my dear, telepathy. I think we should spend a weekend at one of the best north coast hotels."

"What got into you?"

"Say yes and you will find out."

He had never heard so much happiness in her laughter.

"So would you like to go?" he pressed her.

"Sure. But I think you are up to something."

"Better to be up to something than to be down and out, my dear," he said cryptically.

"If I didn't know that you don't drink, I would think you have been drinking something," she said.

"Something remarkable happened recently. I have been sipping the wine of understanding. But I will tell you about it."

"I don't know what it is. But cheers anyway, you Pentecostal spirit-drinker, you!"

"Cheers! And for some reason I am thinking of Byron. He wrote, 'She walks in beauty like the night...'"

In the Garden of Her Names

F***ather, I failed a woman named Miss Violet Dahlia Rose, and I have been trying to make amends and find redemption.***

One year near Christmas I was going through some of the old folders on one of my bookshelves, looking for something or other, when I came upon a large manila envelope labeled NEW POEMS. I opened it and pulled out a wad of yellowing, typed sheets held together by a rusty paper-clip. I flipped through the pages to see if I could find anything of interest, and my eyes fell on the following poem:

Her Christmas Moment

*I found an old card from her which said,
"Two things I like at Christmas:
Poinsettias and Nat 'King' Cole*

IN THE GARDEN OF HER NAMES

> Singing "The Christmas Song".
> Her love of poinsettias was appropriate,
> For her name is a garden of flowers in bloom.
>
> And our sensibilities in tune
> Once burned like Yuletide fires.
>
> And then on Christmas Day
> While admiring poinsettias in the garden
> I thought of her.
> And immediately the radio began playing
> Nat 'King' Cole's "The Christmas Song."
>
> "This is her Christmas moment," I said.
> And I celebrated the surprise
> Of having her appear
> In the fortuities of music and flowers.

Cliff Bento

    Old poems seldom satisfy me. Mostly I wonder which idiot could have written such a thing. But once in a while I stumble on an old piece so good I see my present work as evidence of decline and decadence, and I wonder, sadly, if I will ever be able to scale those aesthetic heights again. This poem was not in that elevated category, but I thought that it was not a bad poem. In fact I didn't feel like changing anything in it, which I often do even with published poems. So after reading the others, I decided to rescue it from the company of its weaker brethren.

    When I wrote it, I had intended to send Violet a copy, but for reasons which will soon become evident, I had not.

For years I had been trying to track down Violet, but without success. She had vanished, apparently without leaving a trace. I had sort of given up on ever seeing her again, but finding this poem gave me an idea. I would send it to one of the local newspapers which published poems on Sundays, and hope that they would not only publish it but, miracles of miracles, Violet, who loved poetry, would read it and get in touch with me. I emailed the poem to the editor, and while I waited to see if it would appear in the paper—I checked the paper eagerly every Sunday morning— I reflected on the Cliff and Violet Story, as I began describing it in my mind.

I first noticed her when she was a student in one of my English classes at one of the rural teachers' colleges. At one level this was almost inevitable, for light-skinned people tend to stand out in groups of mostly dark-skinned persons, and so her yellow-ripe mango stood out against the coffee, chocolate, cinnamon, naseberry and golden-apple complexions of her classmates. In addition she was extraordinarliy beautiful, with green eyes, brown hair which hung to her shoulders, and even, rounded facial features. Indeed it was this African roundness, and her generous shapely lips, which did most to unite her in appearance with her classmates. But the main thing I noticed was the sensitivity of her mouth. Whatever her story was, it was most expressed in the sensitivity of those pretty lips and revealing mouth. While returning the first set of essays, I discovered her very beautiful, flowery name.

I was the staff adviser to the Yearbook Committee, and the editor brought me an article written by her for our consideration. It told the fascinating story of how she persuaded two other art students—visual art was another of her specialist subjects—to lead the pupils at the early childhood school in the painting of a mural on the walls of the stairway which went from the road down to the school. The article was illustrated by two stunning photographs of the completed mural. As a poet-painter, I had also studied visual art, including child art, and was aware of the claims made for its contribution to the creative and mental growth of children, as well as of the philosophical questions concerning its aesthetic value. This project struck me as a work of great educational value to all involved, and I was very excited about it. We published the article.

During her internship year her area-supervisor sent her to me to discuss the study they were required to do to satisfy the requirements for the teacher's certificate. The authorities preferred action-research and had given them some preparation for this kind of investigation, but Violet was not particularly interested in doing a 'scientific' study of some small problem in the management and delivery of her subject. She said she wanted to develop the creativity of her pupils either in English studies or art education. I told her that in my view, in a culture of mimicry such as ours, anything which encouraged creativity and innovation ought to be supported.

She came to my office one evening, and after she greeted me, I offered her a seat on the chair in front of my desk. Her hair was cut shorter and combed back in a style fashionable at the time, the name of which I did not know, and she wore a pink dress made of a nearly translucent fabric with embossed designs, rather delicate-looking black shoes, and she carried a handbag made of plaited palm leaves, which seemed to be a craft item from her home-parish St Elizabeth, which was well-known for producing such items. She studied me with her green eyes and explained her problem.

I pulled a book from the shelf behind me and handed it to her. Co-authored by one of my classmates at university, it was an account of an experiment which put real writers to teach creative writing in public schools in New York. In order to carry out the experiment, the writers had formed a collaborative with teachers of English in the schools, and they had met, planned and carried out the programme. The book was a report on the project. She skimmed through the book while I explained what it was about.

"This looks like something I would like to do," she said.

"There are a few writers in Jamaica and I know some of them. Perhaps you and one of them could collaborate in the teaching of one genre: poetry, fiction or drama. Then write up your report and you have a study."

Her eyes changed into nearly all the colours of the rainbow. "That sounds like something I would love to do!" she said. "But will they accept it?"

"There are two main kinds of studies: quantitative and qualitative. This could be a kind of qualitative study. If you learn more about it, you could come up with a proposal which you could then submit to the authorities. If they accept your proposal you will be off and running." I pulled a book on qualitative research from my shelf and handed it to her. "Don't forget the home address of these books," I added.

"You can trust me." She smiled. "I will be sure to bring them back."

She found a poet at the university who was interested, and together they designed a proposal which they submitted to the authorities. It was accepted and they carried out the project. She received an A for her study. She shared the news when she returned my books. I congratulated her and she thanked me warmly. Her area supervisor also came to my office to thank me for my assistance. "She clearly responds to you very well," she observed. "And both of you look alike, you know. Almost like brother and sister. You would make a nice match! How about it?" she added with a wink.

Father, I will not pretend that I never lusted after the pretty women in my classes. I did. To tell the truth I did so a lot. But as long as they were my students I left them alone. I wouldn't touch one of them, not even with a long stick. But once they walked through the gate of the institution it became a very different story. When I re-met them, now as adult-to-adult, man-to-woman, outside the circle of professional ethics, you never could tell what might happen.

Oh yes. I know about the lusting in your heart argument. My interpretation of that remark is that men simply cannot avoid lusting after women in their hearts. So let us accept the inevitable. What matters is if they act on it. And as I said, I controlled myself in that regard.

Violet graduated and went out into the world. I don't recall that I gave her much thought, until I ran into her in an art galley one summer, about three years later. I turned a corner and there she was in a red dress, her hair falling to her shoulders in that familiar curved style, and standing with legs apart in that now familiar relaxed posture, in front of what I recognized as Seya Parboosingh's painting "In Sorrow". She turned when she heard my footsteps, and when she saw me, she smiled shyly.

I said, "I am not surprised to see you standing so transfixed in front of a painting by Seya Parboosingh. I have a feeling that your paintings are a lot like hers."

"How did you know? I really like her work. They are childlike, direct and deep, and clearly come straight from her soul. I have never detected a single lying brushstroke in a piece by her."

"Have you considered doing further studies in art?"

"Yes, but I don't want to go to a college or a university. I would like to be apprenticed to a real artist. As I was to that poet you suggested. I learnt a lot. That was how artists used to study in the old days."

"As it stands I know more poets than painters. But if I hear about any master-artists who take apprentices I will let you know. And what about English?"

"Even though you wrote, 'Surely you can do better than this!' on one of my essays?"

I laughed. "That was because I expected excellence from you. But I can see that you still have me up in your heart over that remark!"

"That essay was about logic. Not my strength. I prefer literature."

"So study literature. And what are you doing these days?"

"I am a guidance counsellor at a new secondary school here in Kingston. Guidance counselling was my third subject at college. The school is in a rough area. One of the senior boys made a sexual advance at me the other day."

"How did that make you feel?"

"It was very disturbing. I get that on the street nearly everyday, and most times it makes me feel like a piece of meat. But when it comes from someone in your class!

I will make sure never to hang around that school late in the evenings!"

"I think you should do some further studies."

"Yes, but I can't decide what to do. The guidance counsellor needs some counselling. May I come to see you one day to discuss my career options? You seem to have a gift for supervision and guidance."

"Sure! Come see me sometime. I live and work at the same place. Just give me a call." I took a piece of blank paper from my wallet (I always have paper on me in case I get an idea for a poem), and wrote my name and number on it, and handed it to her.

"Thanks. You saw me admiring Seya Parboosing's piece. Which is your favourite piece in the show?"

"Osmond Watson's Hallelujah. It is in the next room. Come let us take a look at it."

We stood in front of the bas-relief done in wood, and whch showed a vertical arrangement of Jamaican faces engaged in ecstatic singing.

"It is beautiful!" said Violet. "What expression!"

"Religious joy," I said. "Perhaps the main kind of joy experienced by our people. He is inspired by both Cubism and the African art which influenced it. And he is a good sculptor as well as a good painter."

"I am going downtown to Sandford's Bookstore to buy some books."

"I will soon be heading home. See you."

"Bye for now."

A few nights later, Violet called. "I hope I am not disturbing your tryst with one of your girlfriends," she said.

"Not at all," I replied with a laugh. "I am, as the song says—'I ain't misbehaving, and I am here alone in my room with my little radio'."

"I wonder how often that is the case! Incidentally, I love to hear you laugh. I remember those belly laughs in your classes. Every time I meet you, I hope I will hear you laugh."

"I regard laughter as sacred."

"That is deep. What about next week Saturday? I will be spending the weekend with a friend not far from where you live. You remember Sandra? She was in our class."

"Oh yes. I remember her. She is married with a family."

"I am staying with them. She or her husband will give me a ride."

"That sounds great. I look forward to seeing you."

"I will be there around 3:00 pm."

"Wonderful!"

When the Saturday afternoon came, I heard when her transportation dropped her off in the nearby parking area, and then her footsteps, oh those footsteps! I would get accustomed to hearing them hurrying to me, night after night, in the months ahead! I turned off the cassette radio I kept on the floor within hand-reach of my bed, and then I opened the door of my studio flat, a simple place with a single bed, a kitchenette and bathroom, a sofa, and my desk at the head of the bed, against the wall and below the brown French windows. Violet came towards me with her brown hair freshly curled—an earlier morning visit to the cosmetologist seemed apparent—and wearing figure-hugging blue jeans, and a pair of the delicate black shoes—this one with heels—of which she seemed to be very fond. Her green eyes seemed serious, but there was a slight smile around her sensitive mouth. We embraced and I was immediately smitten by the scent of an alluring perfume that would define her presence in the months ahead.

I invited her into the flat and offered her a seat on the sofa. She politely refused my offer of a drink. I sat on the bed facing her. After some light chatter I said, "I have been thinking about your situation and your various talents. I think you should do a first degree in English. I am not diminishing the importance of the image in favour of the word, but in several cultures it has been declared that 'in the beginning was the word'. So begin with the word by getting a degree in English. It will offer more prestige and opportunities for promotion. You can pursue the image on weekends and in your spare time. You could become apprenticed to that master if you ever find one."

"I will get an application form from the University of the West Indies. Will you be willing to recommend me?"

"Of course. I have already been thinking of some of the things I might write."

"Like?"

"She has a good command of written and spoken English, and she loves to read books of substance. She is intelligent, enterprising and creative. She is a good teacher, and is especially inclined towards innovation and enterprise. She is of a very sensitive disposition. She could make a good contribution to aesthetic education in the county."

"I can feel my head swelling!" she replied and we both laughed.

It had started, or rather continued, the moment we saw each other, and gradually the air had become thick with the sexual energy between us. I got up and locked the door. Then I stood before her, held her palms and felt the electrical energy flowing between them, and pulled her to her feet. I reached for her lips, and the eager warmth and texture of her mouth told me that we had it. We did not only have it. We had it in abundance. After a round of passionate kissing I led her, my heart pounding, towards my bed.

Spare you the details? Yes, I will spare you the details. But I must mention something which is of great importance to me.

In the next few months I was like a thirsty hummingbird let loose in her garden of names. The erotic connection between us was extraordinary. I was no virgin I can tell you. But with her I felt like an extraordinarily strong and very powerful man, and she reciprocated every flourish of my passionate intensities tit-for-tat. I especially remember the time we made love during a shower of rain. The thick and heavy rain was like a wall of protection around us. Each round of lovemaking lasted the exact length of a shower, rising and falling with it, and this gave me a sense of oneness with the cosmos, it made our lovemaking feel like a micro-version of the macro shower of rain and of the cosmos itself. It was like a religious experience, Father. And it rained and rained and rained as if the sky would not empty itself. And the power kept rising and rising in me. "Was that the sensuous artist or the learned professor?" she asked with a chuckle when it was over.

"I think it was the poet of the spirit, my dear," I replied.

It is true that most of her visits ended with us in bed. How I looked forward to the sound of her footsteps on the corridor! But there were also events which were gradually revealing more of her personality and her life. She came from a business family that appeared to be fairly well-off, but their material resources and interests, did not include the kind of nurturing needed by someone with Violet's gentle, sensitive and aesthetic spirit. She said her mother blamed the timing of her birth for the messing up of her own personal life, and never forgave her. Her father saw his role as a material provider and nothing else; preoccupied with his business interests, she saw him as cold and distant. She was closest to her grandmother who had given—indeed had insisted—that she be given her garden of names, but who had passed on when she was only five years of age. A cold and rather reluctant aunt had been largely responsible for her upbringing. She was surrounded by fairly prosperous relatives, but with her temperamental and value-differences, she did not quite feel that she was one of them, and they in turn tended to reject her as being something of an oddity.

She had had a similar experience of alienation at the college. The colour difference, already mentioned, was a source of much unpleasant, and sometimes quite nasty teasing. Being of a similar complexion myself, I could recall being called dirty names at my elementary school, and my colour is continually being referenced as I go about my life. So I could empathize with this aspect of her experience. It is a universal issue I know. Both colours are historically linked on the island, but in some respects they have experienced it differently. It is fundamental to my point of view that I try not to discriminate against persons on the basis of their biological characteristics.

Violet's alienation at the college, she said, also had some of the class associations. From a business rather than an agricultural, peasant background, which would be that of most (but surely not all) of her fellow students, she found herself able to afford certain things like the beautiful clothes she loved so much, that perhaps would be more difficult to attain by those around her, and so she found herself continually being envied, resented and severely criticized. During the practice of 'ragging' (bullying) which was part of orientation, some of her fellow students had dipped her beautiful clothes in mud and thrown them out onto the walkway of the dorm. Her seniors said they were 'levelling' her.

And so her student-years were largely unhappy ones. She kept to herself and did her work. She maintained her temperamental quietness, hoping, as she had read somewhere, that all quiet things are loved, and that she too would come to be loved for her quietness.

One night she came wearing a shape-hugging red dress and carrying what she identified as a bottle of jackfruit liqueur she had made herself. I had never heard of jackfruit liqueur. I knew, from my childhood, that jackfruits had a very contentious scent that people either loved or hated, and that eating a slice of one was a messier business than eating half-a-dozen of the biggest mangoes barehanded. That Violet could tame one into a bottle of liqueur impressed me. I took two glasses from the cupboard and she poured the drink. "Cheers!" we said as we clicked glasses. Then we resumed our usual seat, she on the sofa and me on the bed.

"This liqueur is excellent!" I said after the first sip. "You seem to be one heck of a cook!"

"I am a creative cook," she replied. "You will have a hard time getting me to roast a breadfruit, but if you want breadfruit-punch or breadfruit crepes, that's me!"

Then there was the rose-story. I am not much of a giver-of-flowers to women, but for some reason women seem to like giving them to me. On a number of occasions when I was ill, my female colleagues brought me flowers. It so happened that I had a pot I had made in a ceramics course in Canada —I had thrown it on the wheel, glazed and fired it myself (with much satisfaction), and carried it around as a souvenir. It was now on the floor beside my improvised bookshelf, and it became a convenient receptacle for these gifts of flowers. One evening Violet brought me a magnificent yellow rose from Sandra's garden, and I placed it in the pot. It made me think of a pop song about a yellow rose, but since I could not recall the lyrics, I was unable to detect if there were any parallels between that songwriter's experience and mine. But I do recall that this gift of her namesake considerably increased the intensity of our lovemaking that evening, and made her especially receptive to my gestures of affection, like playing with her hair.

Later there was the shirt-story which nearly tore us apart. One evening she brought me a very handsome white shirt made of a textured material I liked because it looked as if one would be very cool while wearing it in the hot climate, but which I could not identify by name. It was also the kind of shirt that one wears hanging loosely outside, the kind I like to wear in the tropical heat. "I was walking by a store and stopped to look into the display-window," she said. "As soon as my eyes fell on it I said, 'that is Cliff's shirt! I can see it on him!' So I went in and bought it."

Liqueurs and roses were fine, but giving me an item of clothing as a gift made me feel uneasy. I felt that accepting it would seal our relationship and take it to another level, and I did not feel that I was ready for that. There was something I had not told Violet. I had applied for a sholarship to complete my studies in Canada, and I was awaiting the result of my application. If I got the scholarship I would be leaving the island in a few months. What would that do to our relationship? I had tried a long-distance relationship once before and it had failed miserably. I had no intention of embarking on another. I was in a quandary. I did not want to hurt her feelings. The shirt seemed perfect for me, I thought. Yet what might the consequences of accepting it be?

"I don't think I can accept it," I said.

"Why not?" she said, her eyes rapidly changing colours. I didn't tell her.

"Why would you not accept a beautiful shirt from me? Give me one good reason!"

A wish to further one's studies did not seem to logically entail that one should not accept a nice shirt from a beautiful lady.

"Okay, I will accept it," I said.

She smiled. "It never occurred to me that I would have to come here and fight you to accept this shirt. Really! Please try it on."

I went into bathroom and changed shirts. I looked at myself in the mirror and I had to admit that the shirt made me look like a relaxed, dashing, sporty sort of guy. Then I returned to her so she could give it her own appraisal.

"You look like a man who could be my boyfriend," she said.

"I couldn't think of a higher compliment!" I said, and she chuckled sweetly.

The anticipated letter arrived a few weeks later. I was sitting in the staffroom having a cup of coffee when Diana, an expatriate brunette, entered carrying the staff-mail she had collected from the principal's office. She flipped through them as she looked around, and came over to me carrying a large manila envelope. I noticed that it came from the organization to which I had applied for the scholarship, so I opened it eagerly. The letter was an offer of the scholarship! I was thrilled! It was also a generous scholarship which would cover air travel, a monthly stipend, a clothing allowance, a book allowance, health insurance, and the cost of travel to conferences. I would be able to focus on completing my studies without worrying where the next dollar would be coming from.

I was expecting a visit from Violet that evening and I wondered how she would respond to the news. Would she, like the previous girlfriend in similar circumstances, say, "Congratulations! I will not stand in your way. I am happy for you. Accept the scholarship and go make use of this rare and wonderful opportunity."

I don't have a vivid recollection of how we spent that night, or even how I broke the news to her. What I recall is her sorrowful departure the following morning, her face looking very much like the Seya Parboosingh's apparently prophetic painting, "In Sorrow", that I had seen her contemplating in the art gallery. And I too became deeply depressed.

Had I not received the scholarship I could have transferred my credits to the University of the West Indies and completed my degree there, even if it would have had to be a different kind of degree, since they did not have the academic range of the Canadian university. In that case Violet and I could have continued our relationship to whatever conclusion its inner logic demanded. If Violet and I were married, I think the Canadian university would have been willing to make arrangements for her to accompany me as an independent student, and that would probably have helped to solve some of her career uncertainties. If I did not accept the scholarship that would not guarantee that our relationship would have continued to prosper, and I could have ended up losing both the educational opportunity afforded by the scholarship and her. I told myself that however painful it was for the both of us, it certainly appeared to be in my best interest to head for Canada. "Married you can always get..." says a song.

I now believe that my error was not in going to Canada, but in how I handled the separation. I had not prepared her enough for it. Just telling her I had received the scholarship, and that I intended to accept it, was hard and cruel. I now know that a woman bonds with a man with whom she makes love, and the more frequent, intense and satisfying the lovemaking, the stronger the bonding will be. Violet was a woman who was bonding with me very passionately, and if that bond had to be broken, it should have been done gradually, patiently and with a lot more sensitivity than I showed. That was how I failed her.

I know, Father, that acknowledgement of one's wrong doing is an important part of the process of seeking justice, or healing. I never said it to her, which is why I am saying it to you. But I will tell you how I tried to bring about some kind of compensatory justice.

We had only one bit of correspondence during the next three and a half years that I spent in Canada. At my request she sent me a copy of Evon Blake's *Beautiful Jamaica*, a very informative book to pull from the shelf and hand to strangers when they asked about the island.

I found Vancouver a beautiful and cosmopolitan city with an intoxicating array of beautiful women from different ethnicities to choose from, and before long I was dating one of them. Students at a university are mostly transient beings: they graduate and return to their homelands, they transfer to other universities, they go to where the jobs are, and so on. So I soon had to date another. And another. At the time I graduated I was in a situation with a Canadian that was almost symmetrical with the one I had been in with Violet, and the divisive force here was again the scholarship: this time the contractual obligation I had undertaken in accepting it, to return to the island to work after the completion of my studies. But that story is for another confession, Father.

After a few months back on the island, Violet began looming larger and larger in my mind. In comparison with other women, including some of those in Canada, there had been something about the tuned sensibilities we had shared that now seemed like a picture in a zoom lens, to be getting larger and larger, sharper and sharper, until you have the clearest view possible. And this view told me, she was the woman I wanted and needed.

I went in search of her. My inquiries led me to her sister in a nearby town. I drove there one Sunday morning, and by following the directions, I arrived at a cream-coloured bungalow with a flat roof and a verandah. I was greeted by an older sister, Patsy, who had a clear family resemblance, but who did not have Violet's ethereal, poetic quality. I introduced myself and she said she knew who I was. Patsy invited me into the living room and offered me a seat. I politely refused her kind offer of a drink. I was eager to get news of Violet. Patsy took up a photo album from the coffee table, opened it at a chosen page, and put it on my lap.

"Violet is now married," she said. "That is a photo of her husband. And below it is one of their first child, their daughter."

The man looked very African. The daughter was also darkskinned and resembled her father. I saw no evidence of any of Violet's features in her daughter's.

"Violet is now Mrs Diamond," said Patsy.

"What kind of work does her husband do?" I asked.

"He is an engineer. He has a big job with the government."

We spoke about some of Patsy's recollections of Violet, and of her own career as a nurse. Then I rose to go.

"The next time you are in touch with Violet, please tell her I came by."

"Will do."

As I drove home I felt a bit stunned. It seemed as if my plane to Canada was still in the air when she got married. A similar thing had happened with my first long-distance relationship. But the fact that this one was not an attempt at a long-distance relationship softened the blow somewhat. We were both free persons and each could have gone wherever the wind had blown. So that is that, I told myself. I will just let her be.

But Violet called me the following night. It was the same voice, only somewhat deepened by experience, and I recognized it at once. "I heard you came searching for me," she said. "That is very unusual." It occurred to me that she was right. It was she who had done all the visiting during our affair. "So you can be romantic when you want to be," she added.

"I admit that I can be a romantic man. But I also admit that the speed of your marriage really surprised me," I replied.

"I married on the rebound, as the saying goes. Your rejection was one of many I have experienced in my life, and in some ways it was the worst, for I never expected it. It came out of the blue. So I got married because I wanted to show you that there was someone else who wanted me. Not a good reason for marrying, I know that now."

"I saw the photo of your daughter," I said.

"And I just had the second child, another daughter. It was a very difficult birth. I am now suffering from postpartum depression."

"I am very sorry to hear that."

"And he wants to have plenty children. How am I going to manage?"

"What else drew you to him?"

"He is a good provider and takes care of his family."

"That is a big recommendation. Especially in this country."

"I saw you on your university campus."

"What?"

"My husband is a Canadian citizen, actually he is a citizen of a number of countries, just in case, and during all the troubles here with socialism we migrated to Canada. Shortly after you left. We visited your city and took a bus tour which included your campus. I looked through the window and saw you walking with a Chinese friend."

"Imagine that!"

"These green eyes are always watching you! I always know where you are and can find you if I want to. My question is, what should I be for you now? A friend? That sounds too weak. The sister you never had? What?"

"Just act naturally. I am not going to interfere with your marriage. But I am going to show you that I am not entirely the hard, selfish and brutal beast you have every right to think I am."

"Be careful. He has a jealous streak. So under no circumstances should you call or visit me. But I will write to you."

"Good. And thank you for the communication."

A few weeks later a letter arrived from her. I noticed that the outside of the envelope had the address of the school where she was teaching, and not her home address. In the enclosed letter she explained that this was another precaution againt Mr You Know Who, who knew more about me than she had ever told him. She requested that I reply to her at the school's address, but I should never sign my letters with my real name. She had signed hers "Flower". For the rest of our correspondence I signed mine "Hummingbird".

The letter also contained a poem written by her, the central metaphor of which was being in a deep, dark hole, and experiencing not only a condition of loneliness, sadness and despair, but also a desire to resist all attempts at assistance. My re-appearance in her life, in the poem, was symbolized in the form of a man who entered the dark room, turned on the light, and said it was all right to get up. I was very moved by the poem. It gave me a glimpse of what I had done to her. I replied and reminded her of her artistic and teaching talents.

She replied by sending me a sample of her drawings. They were mainly pencil drawings of river-scenes with rocks and trees. She explained that a river ran beside the small suburban town in which she lived, and that she sometimes left her newborn baby with the helper and went to the river to sit quietly and sketch. Sketching by the river had become her little private sacred place of meditation. She felt stuck, but the running river was always going someplace. The ancient rocks had seen it all, but were still there. She loved the lush greenery in a way she had never loved any spot in Canada.

Along with the drawings, that envelope also contained a smaller one with two small, black-and-white photographs of herself. One showed her working with the mural with the pupils of the early childhood school. She wore what looked like a simple and plain blouse, but a short and richly patterned skirt which revealed her shapely legs. I recalled that her fashionable mode of dress had been a source of torture to the puritanical female lecturers at the college who had tried their best to 'level' her. But Violet had the kind of figure that would find its way out of virtually any kind of covering, even a blank sheet wrapped around her would proclaim it. And she had the kind of cultivated fashion sense that, even unconsciously, would make her pick beauty-enhancing garments. The other photo was a very mysterious one. It showed the student-residence in which she once lived at the college, and it was only by studying the photo very carefully that I saw her small face at the right edge of the building peeking from behind.

I replied with a little discourse on the amazing expressive power of lines alone, and recommended that she study the lines of Pablo Picasso, who could say more with a single line than many painters can with an entire painting. Her own lines, I said, showed a combination of strength and sensuousness, and what seemed to me to be a feminine preference for the round and the ovarian. Echoing Ruskin, I said drawing is a way of knowing. It is also the foundation of all visual art: painting is drawing with colours; sculpture is drawing with clay or marble; architecture is drawing spaces.

Regarding the photographs, I told her I saw them as expressing the two extremes of her personality. The peeking Violet was the vulnerable, shy, fearful shadow of the beautiful, confident Rose, a young teacher leading her charges towards creative educational fulfillment. The photos would become treasured mementos of her, and I thanked her for sending them.

Her next letter was a complete surprise. She had seen a poem of mine titled, "Why The Moon Follows Me" in a newspaper, and had cut it out, made copies, and taught it to her English class (she was a guidance counselor but helped with English from time to time). The letter contained some of the short essays some of the pupils had written in reponse to my poem. Out of the mouths of babes, etc. I was touched by the depth of understanding as well as the creativity of the interpretations that they showed. Many said they identified with my own childhood belief that the moon was always following me, and my adult astonishment of travelling to foreign countries and seeing the same old moon of my own familiar mountain hanging over other people's mountains, and the conclusion I had drawn about it as evidence of a cosmic interest and witness for our lives.

In my reply to her I told her that she semed to me to be that rare thing: a good poetry teacher. She did not, as a famous American poet says somewhere, regard the teaching of poetry as the act of tying up the poem on a chair and torturing a confession out of it, or as another poet said, like squeezing it like an orange until not a drop of juice is left in it. She saw poetry teaching as the verbal (especially oral) sharing of experience among human beings through storytelling. She had shared some of my experiences and reflections with some of her pupils, persons I had never seen and may never see, and there had been some understanding between us. I thanked her for doing one of the nicest things anyone had ever done with a poem of mine.

I had my first book, a volume of poetry entitled *The Sound of the River*, accepted for publication. There was the question of a dedication. I had already dedicated my doctoral dissertation to my parents, and I wanted to dedicate my first major work of creative writing to a person or group of persons who were also of major significance in my life. I have already mentioned that at the time Violet was looming in my head as the most significant of all my girlfriends. So I dedicated the book to her.

When it was published and I received my complimentary copies, she was nowhere to be found. She had hinted that they would be moving house, and that she would also be leaving her job. A few months had passed with no letters or telephone calls. I remembered her warning to me that under no circumstances should I call or seek to find her. So I signed a copy of the book, added the words "The dedication says it all", put it in an envelope and then placed it in the pocket of my car. Since my car was usually near to me wherever I went, I felt it was more likely that I would run into her in such a circumstance.

Good fortune was blowing my way, for around the same time the book came out, I also obtained a job at the university in Kingston and moved there.

One morning I drove to work and parked in the faculty's parking-lot. As I stopped my car a big, spanking, pink SUV pulled up in the space beside me. As I came out of my car I saw that Violet was in the driver's eat. Her well-known green eyes were peering at me from under a new fuzzy hairstyle. She smiled, opened the door and stepped out, as if straight from the pages of a special issue of a glamorous fashion magazine.

"I saw your car and followed you," she said. "I told myself that I would follow you until you stopped, no matter where, and here we are." She came towards me and continued, "I have long wondered what you would do the next time you saw me in person." We fell into each other's arms and hugged and hugged and hugged, tighter and tighter. Until she pulled away.

If we were not in a public place, God knows what might have happened, Father. I kept thinking about her husband. She said he was jealous. Was he a licensed firearm owner?

"I hear you dedicated a book to me."

"Yes. I have your copy here." I opened the car, pulled out the envelope with her name on it, and handed it to her. She tore the envelope open.

"Beautiful cover. Your painting?"

"Yes."

She turned the pages and stopped, obviously looking at the dedication. I saw her eyes change colours. When they looked at me they were wet. "Thank you!" she whispered. She held out her hand and we had a very feeling handshake.

"I have to go now," she said as she returned to the SUV.

"Drive carefully," I said.

"I am a very good driver," she replied.

"Frankly, I am a bit surprised that they succeeded in getting you to learn how."

Her self-deprecating little chuckle turned into a laugh. "It wasn't easy, but they succeeded. Now even taxidrivers can't fool with me!" She started the engine. "And remember, don't try to reach me. Wait until I call you." She swung the big vehicle around expertly, blew me a kiss, and was gone.

At the time I thought my story had ended there, and that my redemption had expressed itself in that blown kiss.

But two fortuitous—almost paranormal events—took place which told me that Violet's impact on my psyche was greater than I realized, and that she was not yet ready to go away. They both came from my bookshelves.

One rainy Saturday I was working in my study, and I got up to pull a book from one of my shelves. As I opened the book, the two previously mentioned photographs that Violet had sent me fell to the floor. I picked them up and looked at them with amazement. My mind went back to the period of the 'flower-hummingbird' correspondence I had had with Violet. The picture of her as an art teacher of young children was especially interesting to me now. Had that experience prepared her for her present motherhood? I wondered. I had recently returned to painting, and it seemed to me that this photo would be a good basis for one. I don't copy from photographs, but an interesting photo can sometimes suggest a painting-possibility. This was what happened in this case. Using the photo as a source of information about Violet's figure, and the location as a source of ideas for a possible setting, and adding some children and child-art of my own resources, research and imagination, I completed a painting—acrylic on canvas—with which I was quite pleased. I told myself that if I ever see Violet again I would give it to her.

This story began with my account of finding the Christmas poem I had written inspired by a Christmas card she had sent during that period of our 'flower-hummingbird' correspondence. After some reflection, I had sent the poem to a newspaper. Was this a case of going against her warning and seeking her out? Frankly it was on my part. But this was also what poets do and are entitled to do. They write poems and send them to publishers. Readers are under no obligation to respond to them. After sending the poem I began waiting. Each Sunday morning I waited for the newspapers to arrive, and the first thing I did was look at the poetry section. For a few weeks nothing happened.

Then one Sunday there it was! And it was printed accurately without a single change or error. I waited for the phone to ring.

Two evenings later, right after supper, as I was settling down to an evening of jazz and The Times Literary Supplement, the telephone rang.

"So I see that you have written a poem about me," said her familiar voice, now with a bit of 'foreign' in it.

"Oh yes!" I said laughing. "I threw out my bait and you swallowed it!"

"I can't talk long. I am in our hotel room and the rest of the family—we now have five children—are downstairs playing some kind of game. We migrated to Canada, to Victoria B.C. where the weather is milder, and we are back home in Jamaica for a little Christmas holiday. I picked up one of the newspapers and saw your very well-timed poem. I knew at once that it was about me. You really are a romantic after all. But Mr You Know Who hasn't seen it. He does not read poetry, only scientific journals, magazines about popular mechanics and the newspapers. But he does in fact have one favourite poem: Longfellow's 'The heights of great men reached and kept were not attained by sudden flight', what he would make of it I cannot say."

I told her about the two paintings inspired by her that I had done: Jamaican Flower in a Canadian Pot and The Art Teacher. I told her I would like her to have them.

"No. There is no way he would allow me to have paintings done by you on the walls of our house. I wouldn't even mention them. But please email me some prints, for I would love to see what they look like. He leaves my email account alone. I saw your email address on your university's website and will send you my comments about the paintings to that address. But please keep those paintings as mementos of me."

"Okay. And what about your studies?"

"I have been mainly devoted to my children. But I took your advice about beginning with the word, and I am now enrolled in the B. A. in English programme at the University of Victoria. I have been reading their literary journal The Malahat Review, and hope to send them some poems one day."

"I know it. It is a good journal. Congratulations! But don't give up painting."

"I won't. And what about you? I don't think you are married for I would have heard. These green eyes are always watching you!"

"I am still unmarried. But I have my eyes on a pretty little folksinger in one of my classes. As soon as she graduates I am going to pounce."

"Don't pounce!" she said with a laugh. "Woo her. Woo her!"

"All right!"

She was still laughing. The genuine mirth in her voice, and the remembered blown kiss, confirmed that I was somewhere in the neighbourhod of justice and redemption.

Thank you, Father.

The Bull

(Excerpts from the found journal of Samuel Rhone)

January 4

Jim and Linda Hardy, my American colleagues in the Department of Mathematics, invited me to spend New Year's Eve with them at their cottage in the foothills of the Blue Mountains. Jim is a full professor and Linda and I are assistant lecturers in the same department. It was our first term at the university, and our professional relationship started becoming a friendship after we kept meeting at the Senior Common Room Club. We shared a love of beer and tennis, and we met there to enjoy both after classes in the evenings. Jim was an excellent player who once nearly made it to the US Open, but Linda and I were little more than beginners. But when it comes to beer I can drink both of them under the table at any time!

Except for a hike there as a boy scout, I knew little about those St Andrew hills, except that they were favoured by university lecturers, especially expatriates, who love their cool climate and spectacular views. I am not big on New Year's celebrations, but the thought of a pleasant evening in the cool hills was very appealing, and I promised that I would be there at 7:00 pm—no Jamaica time! Jim insisted. They gave me directions on how to find Eucalyptus Lodge, the complex in which they lived.

I knew that the road was steep and winding, and not having visited their home before, I couldn't estimate how much time it would take to get there, so I left my flat on the campus a little after 6:30 pm. I want to pursue a career in mathematics, but I am also an aspiring novelist, so I had a copy of my first novel in a manila envelope on the passenger seat beside me (my five complimentary copies had only recently arrived in the mail from the publisher in England). I passed Papine, a crowded little town, and was soon climbing into the hills. The "Watch for Falling Rocks" signs disturbed me, for what could one do if one of these rocks fell on the bonnet of one's car? My brand new white Cortina, bought with a loan, is the first car I have ever owned, and friends joked that I treated it better than some men do their wives! So I prayed to the gods to keep their firm hands on those massive rocks that I could see jutting out of the banks. It was now dark, and I was glad for the darkness, for it allowed me to see the headlights of the automobiles, including some very big ones, that swung with great speed around the hair-pin bends.

My headlights shone on the white, wooden sign with the words "Eucalyptus Lodge", and I turned left into the narrow entrance and drove up the unpaved driveway. I arrived on a big lawn and recognized the Hardy's Land Rover which was parked near a long bungalow on the northern end. There was a big cottage on top of the gradient on my left, but there were no lights in the building. My directions were that Jim and Linda lived in the northern half of the long bungalow, so I picked up the envelope with my novel, locked the door of the car, and began walking towards where I expected to find them.

I could see light in the louvres on my left, and I heard the sound of classical music. I knocked on the door.

"Who is it?" asked Linda.

"Sam."

The door swung wide open and there was Linda smiling, with her black hair hanging to her shoulders, and wearing a stunning purple caftan. "Hi, we're glad to see you, Sam!" she said. I handed her the packet. "A present? You didn't have to bring a present." She opened it, pulled out the book and read the cover aloud: "The Rasta Village. By Samuel Rhone! Congratulations, Sam!" She embraced me. "You didn't tell us that you are a novelist."

"An aspiring novelist," I replied. "This is my first."

Jim had come up behind Linda; he was stocky and blond, and more stoic in personality. "Hi Sam," he said as Linda handed him the novel. "Congrats," he said. "I can't think of many novelist-mathematicians, although there are lots of novels about mathematics."

"Wilson Harris, the great Guyanese novelist, began life as a land surveyor," I said. "And land surveying is a kind of applied mathematics. And Lewis Carroll, the author of *Alice in Wonderland*, was also a mathematician and logician. Nicanor Parra, the great Chilean poet, is a mathematician and theoretical physicist."

"Perhaps you will follow in their footsteps," said Linda. "Please have a seat, Sam. Is it a foregone conclusion what you will have to drink, or would you like to try my sorrel?"

"I will have your sorrel," I said as I sat in one of the wicker chairs.

"And I will have another gin and tonic, my dear," said Jim as he sat facing me.

I glanced towards the open window on my left and the spectacular view below caught my eye. I got up to look at it. "Ye gods!" I exclaimed as I saw the twinkling lights of the largest English-speaking city south of Miami spread out below me beside the sea. "I could live with this," I said.

"It is wonderful company to come home to in the evenings," said Linda as she brought us the drinks. She sat on Jim's left. "I have fallen in love with sorrel," she said.

"Cheers and Happy New Year!" I said as I raised my glass.

"It is a bit early for the countdown," said Jim, "but cheers nevertheless."

"Cheers," said Linda as the three of us clicked glasses.

"We're listening to Chopin," said Linda, "but we have some reggae."

"The reggae can wait," I said. "I am a big fan of Chopin's. One of my dreams is to attend the big Chopin International Piano Competition one of these years. I love playing his music."

"You also play the piano?" asked Linda.

"A little."

"You get around, don't you?" said Linda.

"Just my curiosity."

"Dinner is actually ready," said Linda. "But we are waiting for Maggie, our next-door neighbor. She's from the States, too, from St Paul's. She teaches music at a college in Kingston."

"I don't want to discourage you from writing novels," said Jim, "but they will mean nothing to the Appointments and Promotions Committee. If you don't get some mathematics published they will throw you out. Not even Charles Dickens could get away with writing novels on this campus. And Shakespeare would not stand a chance applying for a job in the English Department."

"I know," I assured Jim. "I already have an article accepted by the Mathematical Intellingencer, and I recently submitted another to the Bulletin of the American Mathematical Society."

"Good. And please feel free to pass anything you write by me. I will be happy to give you my comments."

"Thanks, Jim."

There was a knock on the door and Linda rose to answer it. "Hi Maggie! Come in. We've been waiting for you," we heard Linda say.

I turned to look at the newcomer. She was a chubby, smiling, white woman perhaps in her thirties, with what I would come to know as strawberry-blonde hair, and she was wearing a red dress. She handed Linda what looked like a bottle in a brown paper-bag, and after the usual disclaimer that she needn't have brought anything, Linda escorted her towards me for the introduction: "Dr Sam Rhone, let me present you to Miss Margaret Malone."

"Their surnames rhyme!" exclaimed Jim. "I thought that happened only in poetry."

Maggie and I laughed as we shook hands. Our eyes locked and held, and there was that familiar tension I always feel when I look into the eyes of a woman who is attracted to me. Maggie sat on Jim's right in front of me. "What would you like to drink, Maggie?" asked Linda.

"Some fruit juice will be fine."

"Will orange juice be okay?"

"Perfect," said Maggie.

Linda went into the kitchen and, after serving Maggie the orange juice, returned to her position on Jim's left, with her glass of sorrel held elegantly in her right hand. She picked up my novel from the coffee table and handed it to Maggie, who read the front cover, and turned it around to look at the cover photo. "A novelist! You are my first Jamaican novelist. And a handsome cover- photo, too, even if you don't look like a Rasta. Are you a baldhead Rasta?"

"I believe there is a Rasta in every Jamaican," I said. "We are all manifestations of some aspect of Rastafari."

"That is a very bold thesis," said Maggie. "Would you care to expand on it?"

"That is the idea which the novel explores," I replied, "so you will have to read it to find out what I am saying."

"Is it available in the University Bookshop?"

"Yes and elsewhere."

"I will get a copy, "said Maggie. "Men wearing dread-locks was the first thing that struck me when I arrived here. I find them so erotic!"

Perhaps that explains the Rent-a-Dread phenomenon in Negril and other tourist areas, I said to myself, and for the first time regretted my own 'baldhead' status.

"A bold sociological thesis indeed," said Jim, "even if it comes from a mathematician."

"I find sociology easier to negotiate than mathematics," said Maggie. "So I am not complaining."

"It is dinner time!" sang Linda in a musical voice.

"Let me help you," said Maggie as she rose from her seat.

The dining table was near to the record player, and the women began putting out the meal. Jim mentioned a book he had received in the mail recently which dealt with the question of whether there can be mathematical proofs without words, using visual images only. He wanted to know what I thought about the issue. I told him I hadn't given the topic much thought, but that I was intuitively inclined to believe that there could be such proofs. He offered to lend me the book when he was finished with it.

"Dinner is served!" said Linda, and Jim and I moved over to the table. Jim sat at the head facing Linda, and I sat facing the smiling eyes of Maggie Malone. I don't remember much about the meal, except that it began with a salad eaten first, and not throughout the meal as is the custom on the island, and I believe we also enjoyed ham, turkey and mashed potatoes. There was a specially made eggplant casserole with nut-meat for Maggie who was a vegetarian. For dessert, Linda served the iconic American apple pie, which I was having for the first time. I am used to eating apples raw, and it took me some time adjusting to the idea of cooked apples. But with a scoop of rum-and-raisin ice cream on top of the pie it tasted like 'Jamerican' heaven!

I don't remember much of the conversation, except that Maggie used the word 'penetrating' a lot, for it was clearly one of her favourites: like, "If you asked more penetrating questions you would get richer answers"; and "Do you think your account of the Rastas is more penetrating than that famous one done by Rex Nettleford and others?"; "Wow! that was a very penetrating observation!"

After the meal we retired to the living area for Blue Mountain coffee. Jim put the soundtrack of the film "The Harder They Come" on the player, and the sweet reggae music was like a shot of rum into our Blue Mountain coffee. We agreed it was one of the best collections of reggae songs ever put together. "I hear the movie is shaping up to become a cult film in the USA," I said, and then continued: "I thought it was just the music, but when an American asked me if it is an adults-only movie, I realized that many of them take the title very literally!" There was some laughter. "Did Jamaicans know what they were doing when they named that club in Negril 'The Soon-Come Night Club?' asked Jim.

"I bet they did," said Linda and we all laughed.

After that record was finished, Jim showed that they were very well stocked with the latest reggae hits. He opened another bottle of wine. Reggae music and wine took us up to midnight, and we turned on the radio for the countdown, and the welcoming of 1976. "Happy New Year!" we said, embracing each other.

Shortly after, as if in concert, Maggie and I rose to go. We thanked Jim and Linda for a very lovely evening.

"You must come again soon," said Linda.

"And don't wait until next New Year's Eve!" said Jim. Maggie went before me and I closed the door and followed her. She was standing and waiting for me.

"You are coming with me!" she said as she clutched my left arm above the elbow. She began leading me towards her apartment. I had received many Christmas gifts over the years, but this was the first New Year's gift that I could recall! And it had come so early in the New Year! What a way to get the New Year going! I said to myself as I followed her into her apartment.

She took out her keys, opened the door and turned on the light. Then she turned around and locked the door. She led me across the living and dining area, and I noticed a dining table with chairs, shelves laden with books, wicker furniture, and the large floor-mat, apparently made of local sisal.

"What a lot of books," I said.

"We'll have all the time in the world for the books," she breathed. "Right now I want you to lie with me." She was the first woman who had ever put it to me so directly, and so biblically.

She led me into the bedroom. There was a large green mat on the floor, with a single pillow; I noticed no other furnishings.

"It is my yoga mat," she said. "It is all I need."

She began taking off her clothes. She was plump but shapely, Rubensesque as a painter-friend of mine would probably put it, and her tanned skin was honey-curry-brown, not putty-ish white like that of some of the white women I had seen on our north-coast beaches. I was especially drawn to her full, well-shaped breasts which had the most erotic pink nipples I had ever seen, clearly an example of the kind that drove the European poets mad, and made them reach for vain and clearly inadequate metaphors about rosebuds. I picked up her body scent which I would come to know very well.

Excited, I tore off my own clothes and threw them on the floor. We embraced each other eagerly as my lips found the enthusiastic hot honey of her mouth.

"I am terrified of pregnancy," she said. "The other day I went to visit a pregnant colleague, and she seemed so huge, helpless and vulnerable, sprawled on the bed. I don't want to ever be like that."

"What about contraceptives? I have condoms."
"None is 100% safe."
She probably saw the disappointment on my face.
"So there will be no intercourse," she said. "But I will give you all the outercourse you want."

She played my saxophone. It was the first time it was done to me. Her notes were electrically sweet, and they rose to a crescendo that left me exploded and exhausted.

We fell asleep locked like two spoons.

I did not want to be seen waking up on the premises, so when I awoke at dawn I got dressed and left the house. I descended to Kingston in a white mist.

January 15

I have been thinking about Maggie a lot. I am between girlfriends, so to speak, for my latest recently left for the States to study educational administration. She wanted a long-distance relationship but I declined— I am a bird-in-the-hand type of guy. I haven't ruled out marriage but that will not happen before I complete my PhD, for like publications, it is a basic requirement for university teaching and that is what I want to do. I am the only academically-inclined member of my family: my older brother wants to help my parents with the shop, and my younger sister, who is in high school, dreams of owning a fleet of buses. They can make sense of my interest in mathematics, for they see it as 'useful', but regard my interest in writing as a kind of aberration. "I didn't send you to school to learn to tell Anansi stories!" my father once said. My former girlfriend was no better. Once she asked me what I wanted to do with my life and

I told her I wanted to be a writer. "What a strange thing to want to be!" she had replied. At least she had not cursed the Jamaican badwords I had heard a noted West Indian writer say his Jamaican wife used when he announced his intention to have a go at being a writer!

Maggie is the first white woman I have been so close to, and I know the question of colour will keep coming up if I pursue a relationship with her. It just occurred to me that the previous sentence is only partly true. The first picture of a nude woman I ever saw was of a white woman, and it was on a pen-knife that a cousin showed me when I was a boy; it was a frontal nude and it was the first time I was discovering that women have pubic hair. My first wet-dream starred the blonde girl on a calendar we had in our home. As a teenager, I saw beautiful nude white women in "Playboy" and "Penthouse" magazines; occasionally you would see a black or Chinese girl, but those were rare. Then one of our major newspapers published a photo of a nude white woman once a week (I recall that this caused some controversy). I went to the cinema and lusted after Bridget Bardot and Elizabeth Taylor. Later I saw black American nude women in Players Magazine. Beautiful nude Jamaican women, to all their ethnic extremes, as well as their incredible mixes and varieties, seldom found a media outlet anywhere. I realize that this is sad, no matter how you look at it. Of course my real-life experiences with nude Jamaican women, of nearly every colour, have probably made up somewhat for the absences in my earlier art education, but one cannot underestimate what guys like Freud and Jung might say about these matters.

But in spite of all that I have just said, I consider myself sufficiently intelligent and educated to realize that skin colour is too frivolous a thing to be a major factor in important life-choices of any kind. And unlike some men of colour I know, I do not feel I have any obligation to nationalize or colourize or politicize my intimate personal affections.

Maggie did not have a telephone at home, so she called me one day from a public call-box at her college. "Some men come like a thief in the night," she said, "and others escape like a thief early in the morning! Why didn't you make us wake up together? I would have loved to make you breakfast."

"I didn't feel like hanging around."

"I will give you another chance this Friday evening. Please come for dinner at 7:00 pm. Will that be all right?"

"Sure."

"You may have noticed that I am a vegetarian. Do you have a favourite Jamaican vegetarian meal that you would like me to make for you?"

"I can't think of any."

"And he claims he has written a book about the Rastas!" she exclaimed mockingly. "Actually, I bought a copy of your book and I am reading it with great interest. I will give you a review when you come on Friday."

"That sounds great. It will be my first review. Don't worry too much about what to serve me. I am omnivorous and will work my way through virtually any meal. I have yet to be defeated by a dinner."

"All right. So see you on Friday evening. And don't work too hard. I want you well rested." Her last sentence gave me a little sexual jolt, and I smiled as I told her I was looking forward to seeing her again.

I arrived at 6:45 pm and knocked on her door. "Come in," she said as she opened it. "I am glad you are early." She glanced down at her watch. "We will actually have an extra fifteen minutes!"

"What a flatterer you are!" I said. "As if every minute I spend with you is so precious."

"But they are! I share the Japanese Buddhist view that life is constantly flowing one-way to some vast unquenchable unknown, and that we should grab hold of all the special moments that come our way, and savour them fully and as completely as we can, for by the next moment they will be gone forever, never to return."

"That is not a bad philosophy. You look great. So let me pause and savour it for as long as I can!" She chuckled as I observed her white and clearly bra-les white T-shirt which allowed her breasts to swing and shimmer, her green shorts which showed her shapely legs, and her pair of wooden sandals, or earthshoes, she explained when I asked about them.

"You look pretty spiffy yourself, in those designer jeans, check shirt and shiny shoes."

"Thanks."

"What would you like to drink?"

"I thought of a beer, but I always feel I should be virtuous when I am with vegetarians."

"'Doth thou think that because thou art virtuous there shall be no more cakes and ale?' That's a favourite quote from Shakespeare, I believe. No matter how virtuous some people might think they are, there will always be cakes and ale around. And Benjamin Franklin also said, 'beer is evidence that God loves us and wants us to be happy'. So you shall have your beer. Please have a seat and make yourself comfortable." She went into the kitchen to get the drinks.

I sat down and noticed that my novel was on the coffee table.

Maggie returned and handed me the beer. "Thanks," I said and added: "There is a song my father likes to sing. I don't remember all the words but the opening ones are: 'In heaven there is no beer/ That is why we drink it here!'

Maggie laughed. "I can't think of a similar lyric for my soursop juice—one of my greatest discoveries here—but cheers nevertheless." We clicked glasses.

"So what is your definition of a novel?" she asked. The question took me by surprise, but I rallied as quickly and as best as I could.

"I like Camus's view. He says a novel is philosophy with images."

"And so your novel is the philosophy of Rastafari with the images of rural Jamaican life."

"Exactly."

"That alienation, that not-quite-being-at home-ness on the island, which you say is inside every Jamaican, including every Rastafarian, and which yearns to be somewhere else: London, New York, Toronto, and in the case of the Rastas, Africa or Ethiopia more specifically, is a lot like the universal human suffering and illfare that Buddhists call 'dukkha'."

"Perhaps I should read more Buddhism."

"And your protagonist, the charistmatic Ras Eldread, who converts to Rastafari, and over a number of years succeeds in converting all forty-seven residents of the village to this religion, is one of the cleverest psychologists I have ever come across. It is amazing how he presents a unique version of the doctrine to each individual. He gets the shoemaker to see the making of shoes as the way to African redemption, and the farmers to see their hoes and forks as weapons in a struggle for their liberation."

"Africa is a big problem for every Jamaican," I said "especially since Africans were partners with the Europeans in the slave trade. Yet because of the historical link, no Jamaican can be psychically whole until he makes his peace with Africa. People like Marcus Garvey and the Rastas are forerunners in this regard."

"Very interesting. So are Rastas racists?"

"Some may well be, but none that I know personally. There are white Rastas. And Japanese Rastas. It is becoming an international religion."

"Let's eat!"

Maggie was very much into fruits and vegetables and served two big salads of each. There was a mushroom stew which included tofu, beans, seeds and nuts, which she said were cooked in honey and wine; it was extremely delicious! There was homeade bread, made she said, according to an actual recipe from the book of Ezekiel. I was discovering that Maggie was an interesting blend of Christianity and Eastern religions.

"What made you decide to come to Jamaica?" I asked her.

"Actually I knew very little about the island, except that my mother was a big fan of Harry Belafonte, and I had seen a few ads for beaches on TV. But after I completed my master's degree in music education at the University of Minnesota, one of my professors, who is now a very good friend, saw an ad for teachers in Jamaica and encouraged me to apply for one of the music positions. I had always wondered what it would be like to live in a foreign country, and when they offered me the job I said, here is my opportunity."

"How did you meet Jim and Linda?"

"We arrived at the same time and we were staying at the Sheraton Hotel while the government authorities sorted out accommodation, travel and the like. Someone helped Jim and Linda find this cottage, and they asked me if I would like to join them as their neighbor. One look at the view and I was sold. Let's have coffee on the patio. We can watch the city lights come on. I have a present for you."

"A present!"

"Yes. I am going to serenade you."

"Usually it is the man who does the serenading."

"Well, I believe in equality. Haven't you noticed?"

She opened the door to the patio and I could see that she already had things arranged. There was a chair with her guitar and flute at the far end, a small table for the coffee-pot and cups in the middle, and my chair, that of the serenadee, on the left. As it did every time I looked in that direction, the magnificent panorama of the city and the sea, and the ever-changing configuration of arriving and departing ships, took my breath away. Only a few lights were now visible, but before long they would be thicker than those visible in the sky. I sat down and deeply inhaled the gift of this beautiful setting, and said a quiet prayer of thanks for Maggie and her hospitality.

Maggie served the coffee. Then she sat in her chair with her cup, and sipped the aromatic beverage with obvious pleasure. "Nothing like black Blue Mountain coffee," she said. "You can actually taste the flavour. I notice that, like most Jamaicans, you spoil yours with milk and sugar. But thank God you do not use condensed milk!"

"There is a saying that most Jamaican men like a little milk in their coffee. The reference is to mixed race women," I explained.

"I get it. And no doubt some like a little coffee in their milk. And some prefer their milk straight. Straight coffee may be hard to find on the island. And where do you stand on this matter?"

"I give thanks for all of God's creatures."

"It seems you are a 'sweet-mouth' man. I got that expression from a higgler in the Papine Market."

I laughed, both delighted and amused to hear her use a Jamaican expression with an American accent.

When we were finished with our coffee she picked up her flute. "I am going to play two of Bach's fugues. Many music critics think Bach is to music what Shakespeare is to literature and Newton is to science. They say he mastered everything that came before him, and influenced everything that came after him, including jazz, pop and electronic music. I don't know about reggae." She began playing and I was immediately captivated by her talent and skill. In addition, I detected the rigorous mathematics in the music. Had Euclid been a Christian and a musician, he might have composed music resembling this. I found it the kind of music that made me want to worship and dance at the same time, or perhaps dance in worship. It kept pulling me upwards in thought and emotion. At the same time the music had a sensuousness that could come only from a man who fathered twenty children. When she was finished, I applauded with enthusiasm and gratitude.

Then she picked up her guitar. "I am going to play some excerpts from Joaquin Rodrigo's 'Concierto de Aranjuez.' It is my favourite piece of Spanish music."

If Bach pulled me towards the heavens, Rodrigo made me think of delightful evening breezes and lovely gardens. His musical patterns sounded so rare, they were like those gifts of the spirit that a man is lucky if he stumbles on only once in his lifetime. I listened as his nuggets of gold fell from Maggie's guitar strings.

THE BULL

I had been erotically stirred by women playing music before, like the movement of my Sunday school teacher's legs as she pumped the organ, and whenever I see women playing saxophones. The enjoyment of the music in Maggie's eyes, the light of evening on her tanned skin, and the natural way in which the music poured out of her being stirred something deep inside me, and before I knew what I was doing, I had passed the coffee table, and had reached down and taken possession of her mouth. She moaned, pulled away and said, "I didn't expect this. At least, not so sudden." By which time I had pushed aside the musical instruments, and had pulled her to her feet. I embraced her hungrily and in the wild reciprocity of our exploring tongues. It flashed through my mind that many a filmmaker would pay a fortune for this scene of our passionate lovemaking in this remarkably beautiful spot. "I want you right now!" I breathed as I squeezed her so hard it felt as if all the breath had left our bodies. I felt her grasp my left hand as she began leading me inside.

Within seconds we had both torn off our clothes and were together on the yoga mat.

"I want you so badly," she said. "I wonder if I am safe? By my calculation I should be. But you can't be 100% sure can you? Damn this Vatican Roulette! No, I simply cannot take this risk!"

My feeling was to say to heck with it, mount her, enter her and fuck her golden deliciousness with wild and total abandon for as long and as hard as I could. But if I went against her desire wouldn't it be rape? Many women have lured men to the brink of their wells and, having second thoughts afterwards, had cried rape after he had drunk the water and satisfied his thirst. I have never raped a woman. I have had wild impossible fantasies about it while seeing sexy women on the streets and on beaches and so on. But deep down I don't think I could enjoy it unless I felt convinced that the woman wanted it as much as I did. In fact, I regard rape as one of the most despicable of crimes; to force one's self into another's body without that person's consent is the worst possible form of violation.

During our first encounter, Maggie had said she was terrified of pregnancy. I had not asked for an explanation and she had only hinted at one reason for her aversion. I had no doubt there were deep reasons, perhaps beyond my comprehension. As an imaginative man, I could understand why a woman might want to avoid the pains and terrors of childbirth as well as abortion. To become pregnant and deliver a child is literally to risk one's life. It is also an enormous responsibility. If one has such feelings, beliefs and doubts, sex, even terrific sex, might not seem an adequate reward for the price one might have to pay for it.

So I decided to hold my horses and not overwhelm Maggie by force. There was apology all over her face. "You must wonder what kind of woman I am, always luring you and not delivering the goods. But I do enjoy the other things very much. So I will never have full sex unless the time comes when I feel I want to, and want to very much. I can't go against my feelings and my sense of integrity. Do you understand?"

"My mind does, even if my body is asking me what the hell is going on here?"

She reached over and kissed me lightly on my right cheek. "Thank you!" she breathed. But I grabbed her mouth with mine and kissed it. I felt her body relax as it sank to the mat.

She played my saxophone again. This time it was with even with greater enthusiasm. It was clear that she had acquired a lot of skill at this outercourse business.

Over our breakfast of fruit, oatmeal and coffee the following morning, she told me that she came from a large and rather dysfunctional family, whose living habits she did not intend to imitate.

Although I saw the Hardy's Land Rover parked at its usual spot, I did not go over to say hello. I did not feel I was ready to discuss Maggie with them. So I got into my car and began driving downhill. The mists were already beginning to clear.

February 15

I had a strong desire to see Maggie, so I decided to surprise her with an unplanned visit. I chose a Thursday afternoon since, in order to encourage students to take part in extra-curricular activities, no classes were scheduled at the university for that period. There was bound to be some boring meeting or other planned, but I would be happy to leave it behind me as I headed for Irish Town. In addition, the following day, Friday, would be Valentine's Day, and I wanted to give Maggie a present.

When the day came I set off early in the morning for the Coronation Market which is located downtown Kingston. I bought one of those small, cute, Jamaican-style baskets that I had seen women use for minor shopping in supermarkets, and filled it with seasonal fruits: early mangoes, starapples, otaheite apples, naseberries and ripe bananas. On my way back I stopped at a pharmacy and bought a card in which I inscribed some favourite words of mine from Rabindranath Tagore, with which he urges us to taste the fresh fruits of life, and to sing the songs of life with vigour.

I made it back to the campus on time to teach my classes. Following this I had a quick lunch at the Senior Common Room Club. Then I went home and did some marking. I was used to visiting Eucalyptus Lodge at night, and one morning had caught me there. Today I would get to see what it looked like in the evening. With my excitement building up, I set off at 3:00 pm.

There were no automobiles in the parking area and the place felt empty. I looked closely at the tall Eucalyptus trees that gave the place its name; some people dislike their medicinal smell but I love it. I walked over to the edge to take a closer look at the view. It was the first time I was seeing the magnificent view without any lights at all. I recognized the long strip of the Palisadoes Road which led to the airport and the famed partly-sunken city of Port Royal. There were two ships in the sea and a third was about to enter the docks. I wondered where they were coming from or going. The sprawling city was a mosaic of white rectangles, but with much more greenery than I expected to see.

"Fancy seeing you here at this time!" said a familiar voice, and I turned to see Maggie about to enter the parking area, wearing a white T-shirt, shorts and sneakers.

"Is it safe to jog on these roads?" I asked her. "With all those trucks, buses and army lorries swinging around those sharp corners?"

"I don't jog. I just walk. And you learn to walk facing the oncoming traffic, and to keep well on the left as the signs warn."

"I was longing to see you, and I brought you a Valentine's Day gift for tomorrow." I took the little basket of fruits and card from the car and presented it to her. I watched her eyes changing to all the colours of the rainbow. "You didn't have to. But this is so sweet! And what an adorable little basket!"

She began walking towards the door of the flat and I followed. She took the basket of fruits into the kitchen, and when she came out she said, "I am going to take a shower. Have fun exploring my bookshelves."

As I expected, there were several books about Buddhism and Asian as well as western philosophy, music and music education, including volumes on the great composers, as well as on vegetarian cookery, but this was also the library of someone with a good liberal education, for the titles also included a wide variety of subjects including mathematics and the natural sciences, social sciences like psychology, sociology, anthropology and economics, as well as several titles from the arts including art history, theatre and film. But the majority of the books were novels, for it seemed she had a copy of every classic novel ever written, mainly from the western canon, but there were also novels and poetry collections by African-American authors as well as authors from Latin America, Japan, Africa and Australia. There was a small but apparently growing section featuring Caribbean and especially Jamaican authors. I noted with pleasure that my novel was prominently placed among them.

She returned to the living room wearing a red dress made of some light, thin, translucent material which, as she moved, offered seductive glimpses of her nude form underneath. "Seen anything interesting?" she asked, and noticing my eyes devouring her body she added: "On the bookshelves, I mean."

"Oh yes, indeed! Nothing quite as translucent there, of course, but I was pleasantly surprised to see a copy of Euclid's Elements and other important books in the history of mathematics."

"My friend, the professor of Buddhist studies I think I mentioned before, who changed my life, was also into philosophy of mathematics, and he taught me to appreciate it more than all the other math teachers I have had put together. To him, there is something spiritual about mathematics and that fascinated me. He loved comparing the history of mathematics in the west with that in the east. I am sure you know that the concept of zero came from India and is linked with the concept of nothingness which is so important in Asian thought. And Muslims invented algebra."

"My mathematical education is mostly western, but I agree with you that we should teach our students more about the great mathematicians from other parts of the world."

"I am going to start preparing dinner. Why don't you help me? We could continue our conversation while we prepare the meal. You don't have to know anything about vegetarian cooking. I will give you simple little tasks."

"Sure. I am willing to try."

"And you can sip on a beer while we cook."

Mostly I cut vegetables, mixed batter, and sliced bread. The rest of the time I stood by the door, sipping the beer, and watched as she amazingly created a vegetable salad, vegetable tempura, almond-butter sandwiches, a hearty lentil soup, and a wonderful fruit salad. The conversation we had before she served the meal has remained with me.

"My big dream was to become a concert pianist," she said. "But I have given up on that idea."

"Why?"

"I heard a story about Artur Rubenstein. After one of his concerts a woman said to him, 'I would give my life to be able to play like that'. 'I did,' replied Rubenstein. I am not willing to devote so much of my life to it. So I have taken up making quilts."

"Quilts. Isn't that the thing the Scots wear?"

"They wear kilts, for Christ's sake! Don't be silly!"

"I always mix up those two words. Frankly I am not familiar with either. Tell me more about quilting."

"It is a textile art as old as the Pharoahs. It is a very highly developed art-form in Asia. It also has deep traditions in Europe and the USA. There are wonderful stories about this tradition among American blacks. They used quilts to send messages during the famous Underground Railway which took so many of them to freedom in the north. There is an old joke that Picasso must have got the idea for Cubism from quilting!"

"I have a better idea of it now. But it sounds more like a craft than an art form to me."

"If a novel can be philosophy with images, why can't a quilt be the same kind of object?"

"You got me there! A clean knock-down punch! I need to eat a good dinner before I can recover from that one!"

She chuckled as she enjoyed her debating victory and my response to it. "We'll eat in a few minutes," she said.

Since we had shared the preparation of the meal, even if my role was minimal, the dinner had a special feel of togetherness to it.

"I have something to show you after dinner," said Maggie. "There was no sexual suggestiveness in her tone, so it seemed serious."

"What is it?"

"You will see. I am a more serious quilter than you realize. And I am going to have to work very hard if I want to be as good a quilter as a good concert pianist is."

We were having a very important conversation, getting down to brass tacks as one might say.

After dinner she opened a door to another bedroom that I had not noticed before; it was a two-bedroom apartment. There was a sewing machine in it, and there were textiles and scraps of various colours all over the place. It looked like a much-used and very busy workshop.

"My quilting room," she said.

"Or you could call it your studio," I suggested.

"Thank you."

After she felt we had exhausted our discussion of quilting and art theory, she held my hand and led me to the sofa. We sat down.

"It was very sweet of you to bring me that lovely fruit basket as a Valentine's Day present. And with that beautiful card and that lovely quote from Tagore, someone I also happen to know about and admire. You put a lot of thought into this gift. It is clear that you like me a little."

I put my left arm around her shoulder.

"A lot," I said.

"I have a proposal. Let us just sit here on this sofa and cuddle until you wish to leave."

"Sure."

"Thanks. Not many men know how beautiful just cuddling can be for a woman."

And that was how it was for us for the rest of that evening.

March 23

Maggie called one day to invite me to a performance of their college singers on March 22 at 8:00 pm. The aim was to raise funds for a scholarship for a music student from one of the inner city areas. She would be the accompanist. Jim and Linda would be attending, and she would arrange for them to pick me up at my flat. She had to be at the college early, but would join us on the journey home. I told her that I was proud that she would be contributing to the concert in such an important way, that it was for a very good cause, and that I would be happy to attend. She told me the price of the tickets, and said she would reserve them and arrange for us to pay for and collect them at the door.

Jim and Linda picked me up at 7:30 pm.

"We are pleased that you and Maggie have hit it off," said Linda, as we drove towards the exit of the compound.

"Watch it, Sam," said Jim. "Linda is such a good matchmaker, you will find yourself tied and bound before you know what hit you!"

"The scriptures say it is not good for a man to be alone," replied Linda. "He needs a helpmate. Besides research shows that married men are happier than bachelors."

"There is a saying, Sam," continued Jim: "An unmarried man is incomplete. A married man is finished!"

I laughed loudly at that and said, "You mean that is all the choice we have?"

"That is it exactly, I am afraid," replied Jim. "A man just cannot win. Women have cleverly deluded him into believing that it is a man's world, when they secretly know, as another saying has it, that when the man is born everybody asks 'How is the mother?' When he marries everyone praises the beauty of the bride. And when he dies the big question is: 'How much did he leave his wife?'"

"Did you know that Jim is so cynical, Sam?" asked Linda, turning towards me in the backseat. "Maggie is a nice girl. Going through a bit of a conflict at the moment, perhaps she has told you about it, but I am sure she will resolve it wisely."

"She hasn't mentioned anything."

"Perhaps I jumped the gun. But I am sure she will mention it soon. As her friend I can tell you that you loom very large on her radar."

We were soon close to the college. When we arrived a security guard directed us to parking. We inquired from students until we found the Lecture Theatre. There was no delay in purchasing the tickets, for the lovely young women at the door remembered our names and had the tickets ready. We went inside.

Jamaicans, perhaps in deference to the biblical injunction, tend to sit at the back, while they wait to be invited by the authorities to come up higher, but Linda and Jim, preferring the best seats in the house, went straight to the front row so they could see and hear the best of what was on offer. We sat with Linda in the middle. I looked around and saw that the theatre was about half-full. But people were still coming in. I hoped it would not be a Jamaica-time event, starting half-an-hour late, out of respect for the latecomers. But I had a feeling that Maggie's American sense of time as a valuable commodity could probably have some influence.

I was not disappointed. At the stroke of 8:00 pm Maggie appeared at the left entrance of the stage, wearing a stunning purple gown, and began walking towards the piano on the right. She was followed by the conductor, a thin, mostly bald, bespectacled dark-skinned man in a black suit, and the rest of the choir in suits and gowns. They moved quickly and smoothly into their correct formation. Maggie took her seat at the piano. After satisfying himself that the group was well-formed, the conductor turned to face the audience and said, "Please stand for the National Anthem!" We rose, and the sound of what was probably one of the few prayer-anthems in the world, soon filled the theatre.

The singers began with short, popular classical pieces. Hearing the beautiful music, I told myself that Jamaicans must be among the most musically gifted of the world's peoples. The singers ranged in appearance from the beautiful and handsome young to the gravity and self-assurance of the more matured. The pride and loyalty of the college's graduates are well-known, and Maggie later told me that some members of the group were former students who had graduated many years before, but returned year after year to continue singing. Having demonstrated that they were no slouches in classical music, they retired to the changing rooms, and reappeared dressed in colourful folk costumes. We were then treated to beautifully choreographed Jamaican folksongs, some of which included dramatic and humorous contests between men and women. They retired to the dressings rooms again and reappeared for the popular music session dressed in the latest styles. They took us down memory lane with some of the island's best-known hits from mento, through ska down to rock steady and the emerging reggae. This was clearly the audience's favourite section, for many sang along and clapped to the rhythms. The programme ended with a stirring version of Max Romeo's "Let the Power Fall On I".

We waited for Maggie in front of the theatre. She soon joined us, having changed into a brown pants-suit, and carrying a duffel-bag. We showered her with kisses, embraces and congratulations. I took the bag from her and led the way to the parking lot.

As we drove home in the Kingston night, we dissected and evaluated the show. Jim liked the classical section best, and Linda loved the folk. Maggie said the pop section was the real heart-music of the audience, and that that explained why so many were dancing and clapping in their seats. I said I spent most of my time watching the accompanist. Maggie thumped me playfully on my thigh, and said that for her, personally, it had been very challenging to accompany such a range of genres. More familiar with classical, rock, country and blues, she had had to start learning the Caribbean genres since arriving on the island.

"Maggie, I think you were Irie!" I said. "How many Jamaican music teachers could go to the States and accompany a concert of classical music, rock, country, blues, jazz and all that?" I reached for her hand and squeezed it. She squeezed back and we kept holding hands until we arrived at my flat.

"It was a wonderful evening," I said when the car stopped. "Thanks, Jim. Thanks Linda. And thanks to the star of the evening!" I reached over, hugged Maggie and kissed her on her lips. I got out of the car and watched as Jim turned it around. We all waved as they began driving down the gradient. "See you soon!" I heard Maggie shout.

The following day she called to tell me that she was expecting a visit from an overseas friend, and so would not be able to see me for about two weeks. Her voice sounded strained. "Have fun," I said, partly meaning it, and partly wondering if it might be a small cloud appearing on our horizon.

March 25

I told myself that I would not let my imagination run away with me. It occurred to me that she was not someone who spoke a lot about relatives and friends. In fact, the only overseas acquaintance of hers who had taken some kind of form in my mind was the professor of Buddhist philosophy who appeared to have had a formative influence on her mind. To help put her out of my mind, I began working on a new research paper on non-verbal mathematical proofs, a topic suggested by a question raised in my mind by the book that Jim had loaned me. My thoughts of Maggie were mostly flashes of memory of our times together at Eucalyptus Lodge, tinged now by a question of foreboding concerning how long they would last.

Maggie called to invite me to supper on March 8. Her voice sounded a bit subdued. There had been some developments, she said, and we needed to talk.

I drove up the hill in broad daylight, noticing the jutting rocks, none of which had so far fallen on my car. When I arrived, I noticed the Hardy's Land Rover was parked at its usual spot. The cottage on the left remained closed and silent. I knocked on Maggie's door.

She opened the door wearing an apparently self-made dress made of flour-bag, the clothing of the poorest of the poor on the island, but a current socialist fashion trend, said to be aimed at identifying with the masses. I had seen examples of it worn by presenters and other celebrities on television. Maggie noticed that I was staring at it with a look of displeasure, even of horror.

"You don't like it?" she asked.

"It seems aesthetically well-cut," I said, "and you seem to be a good dressmaker and quilter. But where I come from, in Hanover, only the people who have hit the rock-bottom of life would wear flour-bag-clothes. And if they saw people like you and me wearing them, they would probably think we are mocking and laughing at them."

"So you don't support democratic socialism?"

"I am all in favour of uplifting the poor by increasing literacy and other educational opportunities, by encouraging self-reliance in food production and manufacturing, and by removing discriminatory laws from the books, and so on. But going back to wearing flour-bag-clothes? No way!"

"Anyway, come in. I won't turn you away. Even if you are a reactionary and don't see the value of creating a new visual culture from the ground up."

"'Reactionary'? Now you are into name-calling, the lowest form of argument."

"Sit down and have your beer! Or will it be something else?"

"I can see that you will be pleased that I will be having my usual beer. Red is part of orange, the official colour of the socialist party. Had I asked for the other popular beer, with its green bottle, and green being the colour of the opposition party, maybe you really would have sent me packing!"

"You're silly. I am not taking sides with any political party. As an educator working in the arts, I am supporting the development of the local craft industry."

"I admit it does say something about you and the textile, that you can look so good, even in a flour-bag dress!"

"Now you are coming to your senses. I made one of your favourites: vegetarian stewed red peas with lots of coconut milk, thyme, escallion, scotch-bonnet pepper and vegetables, a peanut punch, and ital sweet potato pudding. I got them from the Rasta cookbook you gave me."

"Sounds irie!"

I enjoyed the meal, but she seemed to eat only dutifully, and she observed me from a loving but detached distance.

"Few Rasta queens could cook as well as this," I said after the meal.

"Thank you. I take that as a great comment coming from the author of a book on Rastafari."

"My research wasn't just academic. I spent a lot of time with the Rastas. And I ate a lot of their food. At first some were suspicious. They don't want any baldheads distorting their beliefs. But I got a good feedback from one of them recently, who said he was glad to see a Jamaican writing about them, since so much of the material coming out, especially about reggae music, is written by persons from overseas."

"Coffee?"

"Sure."

Maggie served the coffee and we retired to the living room.

"So how was your time with your guest?" I asked getting right to the point.

"He thinks the island is very beautiful. It was he who encouraged me to come here, as I think I told you, and he hoped to follow me, but he quickly discovered that finding a job teaching Buddhist philosophy here isn't easy."

"This is not Shakyamuni Country," I said. "This is Jehovah Country, Jah Country."

"Why not Jesus Country?" she countered.

"Because that doesn't sound very convincing. I think he rarely gets a look in. But that is another matter. But back to this friend of yours."

"His name is Antonio Mancini, and he has been my most important teacher and mentor for years. He has been my professor, guidance counselor, guru and best friend. And now he wants to marry me."

"Marry you!"

"Yes. I think he feels threatened by you, and he wants us to do it now, before things get out of hand. He wants us to get married in the States during the coming Easter break."

"And do you plan to have your honeymoon at one of our hotels?"

"No."

"And why not? I am not going to break into your hotel with a gun!"

"Don't be silly. If there is a man in the world who deserves me, it is Antonio. He has done more to educate me and to shape my life than anyone else. Even more than the father I hardly knew. I think you deserve me, too, in a way, but you are not ready for this. You still have many things to do. You have to finish your PhD. You have to decide how much Rasta is inside you."

"I can see that you have it all worked out. With no input from me whatsoever. This man who brought you up in the fear and admonition of himself must have it all his way!"

"You are distorting things! There is no fear. There is no admonishment. Only a deep love and mutual respect. He's the gentlest man I have ever known."

"Okay. I wish you all the best with your Buddhist parson."

"You keep on being silly! Buddhist teachers are not parsons."

"All right! All right! I will cool down. I will cool down. You can't hit me on the chin and expect me to say, 'Thank you! God bless you!'"

"This isn't easy for me either. I do care about you very much, and the feelings increase everytime we are intimate." Her manner changed suddenly, and she continued, "I have observed that you were very interested in the books on my shelves. I may take back a few, but you are welcome to help yourself to as many as you like. I even got some boxes for you."

While she got the boxes I began pulling books from her shelves. I believe that an aspiring novelist should read the great ones, so I helped myself to The Great Gatsby, Moby Dick, The Adventures of Huckleberry Finn, Invisible Man, Native Son, House Made of Dawn, War and Peace, The Brothers Karomazov, Crime and Punishment, Ulysses, The Sound and the Fury, and Great Expectations. I picked some science and mathematics titles too: On the Origin of Species, The Foundations of Arithmetic, Principia, and Mathematics and the Imagination. I also picked some philosophy: The Republic, Meditations on First Philosophy, A Treatise on Human Nature, Buddhist Philosophy, Ethics, and A History of Western Philosophy.

"Only those?" she asked.

"These are fine," I replied.

"I have another present for you," she said as she began walking towards her quilting room. She came out carrying one of the socialist flour-bag shirts. "Please promise me you will take it," she pleaded. "I designed it especially for you. It even has your special symbol."

"Symbol?" I took the shirt from her and examined it. At first I saw only the name of the company that distributed the flour, and the weight of the bag. Then I turned it over and saw that on the back of the shirt was the image of a charging red bull. The bull was part of the fabric, and she had incorporated it into the design of the shirt. "So this is my symbol, huh?" I said. "Some symbol! Are you making some kind of joke?" There was a mysterious kind of light in her eyes. "Please accept the shirt!" she demanded. Without saying yes or no, I threw the shirt on top of one of the boxes with the books.

"I will let you embrace me at the car. Nothing more. I am now bethrothed to another."

When we got to the car we embraced as she wished, and as soon as she felt the desire rising in my body, she pulled away. She walked to her door and turned around, and watched me as I drove away from Eucalyptus Lodge.

When I arrived at my apartment I put away the boxes of books. I would unpack them some time later. I put the socialist flour-bag shirt with its image of the charging red bull in the clothes closet. I had no intention of ever wearing it.

January 10

One evening after finishing supper, I was on my way to the sofa to turn on the TV to watch the evening news when my telephone rang. I sat on the sofa and picked it up. I wasn't expecting any calls. I said, "Hello."

"May I speak with Professor Sam Rhone," said a woman's voice.

"Speaking."

"Don't you remember my voice?" asked the speaker with some disappointment.

"I can detect that it is a voice I once knew very well, a long time ago, but one to which I have become so unfamiliar, it is now difficult to place it exactly."

"This is Maggie Malone."

"Maggie? My Maggie? From Eucalyptus Lodge?"

"The same one."

"Ye gods! Where are you calling from? Minnesota?"

"No. From the Pegasus Hotel right here in Kingston, Jamaica."

On hearing those words I felt a slight sexual surge. After nearly thirty years her voice still had the power to do that to me.

"Will I be able to see you?"

"That is why I came. I also wanted to see some of my friends from the college. It will be a very short visit. I have a proposal. May I come to visit you on New Year's Eve? I have become a bit sentimental about you and New Year's Eve."

"What about your husband?"

"He died three years ago. He was much older than me. I did my research. I know you got married and that your wife, Lorna, passed on, also three years ago. I wasn't able to get any information about children."

"We have two girls. They are both studying in the USA."

"I won't bother to ask if you have any current romantic entanglements. They would be irrelevant for my purposes."

"It turns out that there is no serious one at present."

"Please give me directions to your house. You don't need to pick me up. I have a good taxidriver."

I gave her the directions.

"I will be there at 8:00 pm," she said. "Stay rested! Very rested!"

This felt like a gift from heaven. I had been sexually inactive since Lorna's passing. My urologist told me that my testosterone level was lower than normal, and he gave me some injections. The erections returned and they seemed quite hard to me, even if I had not tested them with actual intercourse, or, given Maggie's history, outercourse. For the next couple of days I had an erection every time I thought of Maggie Malone.

She didn't say if she was still a vegetarian, but on New Year's Eve I blew my pension to smithereens by stocking up on fruits, vegetables, peas and beans, nuts, cheeses, eggs, cereals, coffee, smoked salmon, pasta, bread and wine. I got a haircut and a massage. I pulled out some of my favourite CDs, including Ravel's "Bolero" which is said to be of the ideal erotic length. I ate a good supper, put on some music, and waited.

Her knocking on my door sounded like the beating of my heart. I opened the door to see the familiar round face, smiling eyes, strawberry-coloured hair, and a heavier fuller body. She was carrying a duffel-bag, obviously intending to stay for the night. I have almost no recollection of the clothes she was wearing. But her familiar body scent hit me at once, and I felt as if we were heading for her yoga mat. "Fancy seeing you here!" I said, "and on New Year's Eve! You really are a sentimental and romantic woman!" She laughed the laugh I remembered. As she came through the door we embraced, and I felt the fires returning quickly. "I owe you a fuck," she said in a thick voice, "and I have come to give it to you. I don't want to risk any off-putting preliminaries. So let's get down to business!"

I led her into the bedroom and turned the ceiling light on low. We tore off our clothes. Her breasts were bigger but still shapely as if she had not given suck to babies. Instead of making her look less attractive, her fuller, heavier body only made her look more human. Her pubic hair seemed darker. We embraced hungrily, her body scent pulling more and more memories out of me. "I am past menopause so I can't get pregnant any more," she breathed, just as I was about to retaste the hot honey of her mouth. I squeezed her bum and she moaned.

She pulled herself from me, pulled the bed-spread down, and lay on her back with her knees up. "Come enter me!" she pleaded. I remembered her frequent use of the word 'penetration' the first time we met. By the mercy of God I now had a hard erection, so I mounted her and plunged into the thirty-odd years of her waiting wetness. The long yearn for penetration completed, I began thrusting hard, but not too hard for fear of premature ejaculation. "Thanks for not forcing me at Eucalyptus Lodge," she breathed. "I feel it was worth the wait. Do you still have the socialist shirt with the red bull?"

"Yes..."

She continued, "In my fantasies all these years I have imagined you as that charging bull about to mount its longed-for heifer. Now you are that bull, and you have just mounted me." As a boy in the country I had once seen such an explosion of sexual power and energy on a grassy field. I searched for something like it now in my memories of all that unfulfilled outercourse on the yoga mat at Eucalyptus Lodge. It was that golden delicious Maggie in my mind that I heard scream as our union was completed.

We both fell into a deep sleep. When daylight entered the bedroom and the pea-doves began to sing, we had our pillow-talk.

"How did the quilting go?" I asked.

"Very well. Right now I am having a show in an art gallery in St Paul's. I will send you some photos. My artistic future is in that city. Quite a few journals have published articles on me and my work. They range from housekeeping journals to academic periodicals, ones which are strictly about art."

"Have you bridged that concert pianist-quilter divide?"

"Maybe not quite, but I am moving in that direction. I looked you up on the Internet. I saw only two novels but a lot of mathematics."

"Jim was right. The university gave me an ultimatum. They said they had hired me to teach and research mathematics, not to write novels. I fought them for a while. But I do not believe I have it in me to be a martyr for art. Like Vincent Van Gogh. I am told that even professors of English dare not write novels. They have to write literary criticism."

"I am sorry you gave up on your creative writing. I believe you have talent. Perhaps now that you are retired you will take it up again. I am going to keep prodding you in that direction."

"Thanks. I have published quite a bit on visual proofs in mathematics. They are even citing me in publications on the philosophy of visual art. I regard mathematics itself as a human construction, a kind of exact art. Perhaps I should attempt something on quilting. Perhaps we could collaborate on a paper one day."

"It would be wonderful if we could also meet in this way. I teach you quilting, you teach me maths."

"Who would have thought…?"

"I saw that you got your PhD from the University of Michigan. But you returned home and stayed. Does that mean you don't have the Rasta complex you once theorized about?"

"That is an excellent question. Perhaps I don't have it. But I don't think I should pretend to be sure about it. There is seldom a day when I don't wonder how things might have turned out had I remained in the States, or had I migrated to Canada. I certainly wouldn't claim to feel 100% at home in this environment."

"So you are still working on it."

"I think so."

"Any news of Jim and Linda? I lost touch with them."

"They bought a cottage on the north coast. I see them nearly every summer."

"Please say hi to them."

"I sure will."

She snuggled up to me, and I remembered what she once said about cuddling. I began cuddling her. "You are quite a woman to make love to," I said. "Oh my God!"

"All thanks to you, Samuel."

"Did your husband ever penetrate you?"

"No. Few people will ever understand this. But our marriage was about a lot of other things. On the inside it was about spiritual mentorship, intellectual companionship, a very deep friendship and caring for each other, and a great deal of love and mutual repect. But neither of us wanted pregnancy. And we are both opposed to abortion. So it seemed to us that outercourse, not intercourse, was the safest and best means of physical expression."

"I have never heard of one of those. Ye gods! So am I your first?"

"That is not something a woman should say to a man. It would give him too much power over her. So I will neither confirm nor deny it."

I looked into her eyes. They were smiling mysteriously. We made love one more time. But this time it was more in the manner of a denoument. As the afterglow was fading she said, "Let's have breakfast. I can't recall ever being hungrier."

I let her shower and change first. Then I did the same.

She told me that she still preferred vegetarian meals, but was not strict about it. We had a fruit salad, oatmeal, smoked salmon with fried eggs, and some Blue Mountain coffee.

"When do you leave the island?" I asked her.

"My flight is tomorrow evening."

"That soon!"

"My mission is accomplished. You make a very nice bull, I must say. I now know what I wanted to know."

After breakfast she called her taxi driver. "For heaven's sake please return to writing novels," she said. "Presumably your philosophy is still in you. And how can it thrive without its images?" Her cellphone rang. It was her taxi-driver at the gate. We embraced. It was a long embrace. And when she felt the heat of my sexuality rising she pulled away from me gently. "Until you hear from me," she said with a look of regeneration in her smiling eyes.

The Retablo

Dear Juanita,

I am settling in at Thankful Hill quite nicely. It is a rural district in the hills about 25 miles from Kingston. Although most of the country is now in the grip of a terrible drought—after more than 50 years of independence the island's water storage capacity is pretty much that which was left by the colonial government—these hills remain lush and green, and the river in the valley is still flowing; this is largely the result of the conservation techniques introduced, and fiercely monitored, by a retired headmaster who will not allow the people to cut down trees and use the slash-and-burn method of preparing land for farming. The water problem exists, I am told, because the politicians believe they will win more votes by trucking water to affected areas during times of drought, than by building new dams and reservoirs! The manse in which I live, a fairly comfortable three-bedroom bungalow, has a tank which stores rainwater collected with gutters on the roof, and each evening I use a hand-pump to lift water up to the storage tank on the roof which then gravity-feeds it to the house. There is electricity, thanks to a rural electrification programme which (thank God!) both of the two main political parties seem to agree on. The people here are mainly small farmers, higglers (women who take produce to the markets in Kingston), tradesmen, and crafts-women who make items from straw, bamboo and roseapple (baskets, hats, mats, handbags, belts and so on) which they take to Ocho Rios to sell to tourists. The mornings are misty and cool, and no matter how hot the days are, it gets cool enough for comfortable sleep in the nights. You may wonder about the name. After Emancipation, many of the freed slaves sought freedom and independence in the hills, and they gave the most beautiful, poetic and optimistic names to the places where they settled. A rich planter bequeathed this piece of land for the building of a church, and the grateful residents named it the Thankful Hill Church, and the church eventually gave its name to the community.

I was told that the Methodist church here seldom puts its new theology graduates in charge of circuits, so I should be honoured that they have this kind of confidence in me. It could be because I am a bit older than most of my batchmates, or maybe they were impressed that I completed my Licentiate in Theology along with my degree and diploma. Whatever the reason, I am in charge of a circuit of five churches scattered across two parishes. I conduct the communion service at Thankful Hill on the first Sunday of each month, and then do the same at the other churches on a rotating basis. I have a car, a tough little VW Beetle which can do everything except climb trees, and it is ideal for the winding roads. It is said that when asked by the king and queen of Spain to describe Xaymaca, the island that would become Jamaica, Columbus crumbled a piece of paper and placed it on the table in front of them. That pretty much sums up the Jamaican interior, except that it has a thousand shades of green, and there is almost always a mountain in sight. I enjoy travelling through the countryside, and passing through these villages with their poetic names. The church itself is made of cut-stone, and earlier building technique they should probably consider returning to. It has a balcony and a beautiful stained-glass window which I think you will love. When you come I hope you will do a study of the island's stained glass windows and write a piece, perhaps a series, for one of the island's newspapers or magazines. So far I have not seen anything on this aspect of the island's religious art.

    I have a household helper, Miss Ina, a tall, dignified and very able woman who takes very good care of me. But when she is gone the nights are lonely. I lie in bed listening to what sounds like hundreds of crickets, frogs, and probably numerous other un-named insects who are unheard and invisible in the daytime, but who break loose with the wildest of abandon at nights. I can't wait for us to get married so you can join me here. What I wouldn't do to hear your footsteps in this manse, and seeing your beautiful brown eyes looking at me across the dining table at breakfast each morning!

As you know, the island is probably the best-known little country in the world, primarily because of its prowess in sport, music and tourism, and Jamaicans are very proud of what they call 'Brand Jamaica'. But if you ask me, this 'brand' is besieged by so many demons they are going to have to fight very hard to maintain its lustre. In spite of its many assets—fertile soil, good water, excellent climate, stable democratic government, and its enviable freedom of the press—-it remains undeveloped with one of the highest murder rates in the world. The national debt is one of the highest in the world. As I write their dollar is sliding like a downhill skier. Jamaica's position on the United Nations Human Development Index is following the dollar downhill. There is a lot of doubt and pessimism in the country (migration of skilled people is again increasing) and a lot of people seem very quarter-hearted, at best, about their Independence celebrations. One of the island's sociologists has dubbed it 'the confounding island'. Its stagnation is a puzzle to the philosophers of development.

I believe the story I am going to tell you will be of intertest to you as an art historian. It is of considerable interest to me as a Jesusian, the name you know I prefer over Christian. If Jesus had intended to start a new religion, instead of reforming Judaism, which is what some believe he really intended, I wonder which name he would have chosen for it. Certainly not Christianity. They dubbed him with that title 'Christ' long after his lifetime.

The congregation of Thankful Hill is made up of about 95% women. It is well-known that women are more religious than men so this is a worldwide phenomenon. The small group of men who attend our church regularly are mostly older men with feet partly in the grave. The exception is Jerome Lazarus who is youthful looking, although I am not sure what his actual age is for I have never asked him. He is slender and light-skinned, has thoughtful eyes, and wears mostly blue suits. He is seldom absent, sings the hymns fervently, follows the scripture readings, and appears to hang on every word of my sermons. One Sunday as we shook hands at the exit he looked straight into my eyes and said, "I want to know Jesus". It seems to me that he is someone who is after the kind of inner transformation I regard as religion.

For about two or three months I noticed that he was absent and I asked about him. Mrs May Buchanan, one of our most devoted class leaders, identified herself as his aunt—he has two other aunts who attend this church—and reported that he had been in the hospital, but was now back at his home.

"I hope the illness isn't serious," I said.

"It is an old problem, Rev.," she replied. "Him trouble with him head, you know. He has gone to Bellevue before."

"Please give him my regards, and I hope he will rejoin us soon."

One Monday morning Miss Ina outdid herself in preparing breakfast. She served one of her best ever versions of ackee and saltfish, the national dish, accompanied by slices of roast breadfruit, avocado and homegrown coffee. It was preceded by a fruit plate consisting of slices of papaw, an orange and a ripe banana. Very satisfied, I complimented her and rose from the table and went into my study to take care of some administrative matters. Before long there was a knock on the door, and I heard Miss Ina say, "There is a gentleman here to see you, Rev."

"Please send him in!" I called back. A few moments later, Jerome Lazarus entered the study.

"Mr Lazarus! How good to see you!" I said as I rose from my chair and shook his hands. "Please have a seat."

"Thank you," he said and sat down.

I noticed that he was carrying a large, flat parcel which he rested on his lap, and which was now leaning against his stomach and chest. The evidence of sickness was still visible in his eyes, even if they were sufficiently shiny to indicate that better health was on its way back. He wore a white shirt and navy-blue trousers.

"I missed not seeing you in church. Mrs Buchanan told me you were ill."

"It happened before. I felt like someone was stealing my soul. I thought it might be the Devil. They took me to the hospital and I recovered. Then a few months ago it struck again, this time much worse, and I felt that this time I was a goner. My family hired a car and took me to the hospital. The medicine seemed to be even better, for not only do I feel better, but the side-effects are less terrible."

"I think you need to keep taking the medication. As far as I know these illnesses cannot be cured, but they can be controlled. Like diabetes and hypertension. But you have to keep taking the medication or you could have a relapse. The illness will go into remission but it is still there sleeping, and something could wake it up."

"Well, I feel delivered and I did this painting." He removed the brown-paper wrapping and handed the work of art to me. It had been done on some kind of hardboard, perhaps Masonite. "Read the back first," he said. I turned the painting over and saw that, in his angular cursive, he had written the following words: "Received from God Almighty, with thanks, deliverance from the possible fate depicted in this picture. Signed: Jerome Stephen Lazarus."

"You painted a receipt to God acknowledging the healing you received from him."

"Yes."

"It is a retablo."

He stared at me with his eyes showing no recognition of what I had said. He seemed to be waiting for an explanation.

"In Latin American art there is a tradition of people making these kinds of paintings, and they are usually addressed to Jesus or the Virgin Mary. I am a Belizean, as you probably know, and my fiancée, Juanita, is an artist. She has a degree in fine arts from a university in Mexico. I remember her telling me something about retablos."

"Well I don't know anything about Mexico, except that they play football. I draw and paint naturally, and I have been doing it all my life. And doing this painting just seemed like the right thing to do."

"Perhaps the retablo impulse is universal, and expresses itself in different ways in different places," I said.

I turned the painting over. It showed a light-skinned man, with some resemblance to Jerome himself, dressed in rags and lying in a gutter. People were walking on the sidewalk, passing him without showing the slightest interest in his condition. I noticed with a pang of shame that one of the men was wearing a grey suit and a Roman collar, so he was obviously a cleric. A woman who was wearing a blue dress and a cross around her neck, appeared to be a deaconess. The others were ordinary city-folk of varied sizes, shapes, dress and gait. It clearly seemed like a version of the theme of The Good

Samaritan. Then my eyes moved to the right of the picture which depicted a pack of school children in their uniforms of blue-and-white and khaki. I noticed with horror that they were throwing stones at the man in the gutter. There was no redeeming Good Samaritan in this story. Except the God it was addressed to. And perhaps he had come to me seeking some kind of Good Samaritan substitute. The painting was a portrayal of a horrible reality I had read about.

"You are thanking God for saving you from the possibility of this horrible fate," I said trying to make sure I was interpreting his painting correctly.

"Yes."

"God knows everything So he already knows that you have thanked him with this picture. So why are you bringing it to me?"

"It doesn't feel quite finished. You are a man of God, so I feel you might be able to tell me what to do with it. There is nobody else in the district I could ask. I don't feel the headteacher would know. Neither the Justice of the Peace. Certainly not the police."

"Leave it with me," I said, "and I will think about it."

"Sure. Thanks." He began getting up out of the chair, but I felt a desire to get to know him better.

"Would you like some breakfast? Miss Ina could make you something."

"I had breakfast before I came."

"Another cup of coffee won't do you any harm. We also have cornmeal pudding and ice cream."

"Ice cream! I can't say no to ice cream!"

"So let us go into the dining room." I led the way.

Miss Ina served our guest a dish of rum-and-raisin ice cream and gave me a cup of coffee. We sat at the dining table facing each other. Jerome attacked the ice cream with such relish it was clear that the joy of life was returning to his system. I sipped my coffee.

"What kind of work do you do?" I asked him.

"I am a carpenter. My late father, Walter J. Lazarus, taught me. He said he travelled by horse-and-buggy to Kingston to learn the trade from one of the best construction companies on the island. And of his four sons I am the only one who followed in his footsteps. This pleased him very much. One brother is in the States, and two are still here, one is a farmer and the other is a sign-painter. My three sisters migrated to the States. One died and the other two are still over there."

"And what about your mother?"

"When I was seven years old she left the island to join my father in England. I remember that I was going home from school one Friday evening and she met me on the road. She hugged and kissed me and I was surprised for she had never done that before. That night while I was fast asleep she left the district in a hired car. She kept quiet for she didn't want people in the district to know, for they can be envious and bad-mind, and you never know what they might do to stop you. But Gracie, my older sister, knew and she told me the following morning. I went up to the road and sat on the bank all morning as I watched the sky for the plane that was taking my mother away from me. Gracie kept calling me to come for breakfast, but I kept telling her to put it up. I didn't want to miss the plane. It was very late in the morning when I saw a plane, made of aluminium, but it looked smaller than a finger of banana, and had a big sound following it. How could such a little thing carry people? I wondered. Was my mother in it? I couldn't be sure but I convinced myself that she was in it, just to make sure. So I waved her goodbye. The plane moved towards the big mountain on my left, then it went behind the mountain, the noise lessened, and soon I couldn't hear a thing. To this day every time I hear a plane passing overhead I look up at it and remember that morning."

"Is she still alive?"

"Yes. My father came back from England first. He was here alone for many years, then one day I saw him adding on a new bathroom to the house and he told me that my mother was coming back home. He passed away shortly after their reunion. She is now suffering from senility. She doesn't even know who I am. She is again very far away, travelling, almost like being on that plane going to another kind of foreign."

"And how is the carpentry business these days?"

"Not good at all. But I get a job building or repairing from time to time. I have done a lot of voluntary work building coffins and vaults, in the days when that used to be partly the responsibility of the community. But times have changed. Most people now prefer the commercial coffins they can buy from the funeral homes, and they hire a carpenter or mason to build the vault. So sometimes I get a job doing that."

"What about your medical expenses?"

"My relatives give me a little help when they can. Thanks for the ice cream."

"You are very welcome."

"Each time I get paid for a job, the first thing I do is reward myself with an ice cream treat."

"It is a good habit to learn to reward oneself for things accomplished."

"Bye Rev.," he said as he began walking towards the door.

"Goodbye Mr Lazarus. And please feel free to drop by and talk whenever you feel like it. When Juanita comes I am sure she will be very interested in seeing your art. And in the meantime I will try to decide what to do with the retablo."

He began walking down the driveway with some of the reputed shuffle of the mentally ill still evident in his walk. He was at the gate when the sound of a passing plane could be heard overhead. He stopped, looked up and watched it for a while. Then he continued walking down the road.

I went into my study and picked up the retablo. The style was what you might call primitive or intuitive, with dark, heavy, stained-glass-like lines reminiscent of Rouault, one of your favourite painters. After studying it for a while, and sensing the loneliness and horror of the scene as it would be experienced by the mentally ill man, who perhaps had children of his own the same age as those now stoning him, I looked for a place to put it where I could view it from a distance. You have always told me that you need to see a painting from a certain distance in order to fully appreciate it. I placed it on top of a bookcase which faced my desk, and then I sat down and contemplated it. I understood why one would want to thank God very fervently for deliverance from such a horror.

Joel and his retablo had presented me with a moral and professional problem. Our obligations to the mentally ill is a major moral issue. This has been so over the ages. And terrible things have been done to them throughout history: thrown into snake pits; put on ships and put out to sea; and put to death in gas chambers by the Nazis. The Gospels report Jesus casting devils out of people, and some believe these so-called devils were actually mental illnesses. Some see the confessional of the church as the precursor of the psychiatrist's couch. Mental illness has since been medicalized. I did some counselling as a part of my studies but I am no psychiatrist.

I consulted some of the books on my shelves, Pascal said madness is so widespread among mankind that not to be mad would itself be a kind of madness. Some see madness as a healthy response to a sick society. And there seems to be links between madness and genius. Painting had Vincent Van Gogh, poetry had Holderlin, music had Beethoven, science had Isaac Newton, mathematics had Georg Cantor, and politics Winston Churchill. I read that the list includes some 40% of the most creative jazz musicians, including Jamaica's Don Drummond. Were there any mad theologians? I need to do some research on this. According to Foucault, the presence of art is an indication of the absence of madness. This made me think of Joel.

But what should I do with this retablo? Hang it in our church? I hesitated doing this for Jamaicans react very boisterously to public art they do not like. This happened with statues of Bob Marley and Marcus Garvey. The question about what kind of art should be regarded as religious could stir even deeper emotions.

Jerome had passed the moral and theological buck to me, and I decided to pass it to Rev. J. Harold Jenkins the superintendent of our district. I had a scheduled meeting with him to discuss how I was doing at Thankful Hill.

When the day of the meeting arrived, I left home early after Miss Ina's breakfast of cornmeal porridge, harddough bread, slices of paw-paw and instant coffee with condensed milk. I admire the Jesuit practice of not wearing religious garb in ordinary life, so I mostly wear the guayaberas I used to wear there in Belize. Medical doctors wear them a lot here so I often get addressed as 'Doc' on the streets.

I got into my VW Beetle and set off for Kingston. I had Jerome's painting wrapped and resting on the seat beside me. Someday I will share more of my views on how driving on its roads is a symptom of its many historical neuroses, complexes and pathologies. It is the best exhibition of the country's cutthroat individualism. Driving behind another vehicle is seen as a form of humiliation, so each driver thinks he must overtake at all costs, and with poor spatial reasoning, he — it's mostly a he — cannot get back into the convoy resulting in horrendous collisions and a shocking annual rate of road fatalities. If you stop to let a pedestrian cross the street, a nasty homophobic obscenity will be hurled at you. Overtaking around corners is frequently seen.

I descended from the cool hills into the kind of traffic I have just described, and managed to find parking not very far from the superintendent's office. On my way there I saw a man in rags lying on the sidewalk with hs eyes closed. He was probably mentally ill, like Jerome, and probably not. I was not wearing a Roman collar and therefore I was like a cleric in disguise, but I passed, very self-conscious of being a bit like the priest and Levite in the parable of the Good Samaritan. I remembered reading about an experiment at a university in the States where they found that students from the divinity school were more likely to pass a man feigning sickness or death lying on the ground, than students from other faculties at the university. That Jesus of Nazareth was a psychologist. In self-defence, I have often called charitable organizations when I saw bodies lying on the street, but the answer is always the same: they do not have the resources to respond to all such calls. Our cruelty? Our poverty? Or a mix of both? I glanced at my watch. The superintendent was already waiting. I sent up a prayer for the man on the ground, and asked forgiveness for my moral insufficiency. And then hurried to keep my appointment.

"Welcome Brother Fernandez!" said my boss as he rose to shake my hand. He was stocky, dark-skinned and had a round face; specks of grey hair were beginning to show in his hair. He was wearing a dark suit and a Roman collar, and I noticed that his eyes moved over my attire with some disapproval. "Please sit down. How is Juanita?"

"She is fine. She is teaching art a high school."

"When is the wedding?"

"Next year."

"An unmarried minister will soon be a trouble to himself and to the women in his church."

I laughed and said, "I am too busy to be any trouble to myself or to others. And how are you doing?"

"I am busy planning our big crusade to be held at the National Arena. I hope to rope you in."

"Sure."

I opened my briefcase and pulled out my papers. I notice that he was staring at the packet with the retablo which I had placed on his desk.

"There is a story in that packet," I said, "but I will tell you about it after we are finished with the day's main business." I handed him a copy of my typed report.

The details of that meeting need not concern us here. It was nearly midday when we wrapped things up.

It was at that point that I told him about Jerome Lazarus and his retablo. He followed my narrative with obvious interest, and when I opened the packet and showed him the painting he gasped: "Oh my God! What a horrific picture! And what a terrible but beautiful tale." He took the painting from me so he could examine it more carefully. "I empathize with this young man," he said. "Recently I went to a hospital for a minor operation, a hospital from which a number of my family, friends and colleagues did not come out alive, even after minor operations. By the grace of God I came out alive, and here I am trying to do the work I was called to do. I can't paint a retablo, even the word is new to me, but my knees are my retablo, and I did go down on them with thanksgiving." The office was air conditioned but he took out a large white handkerchief and wiped sweat from his face.

I told him about the man I had just seen on the ground.

"You should go downtown," he replied. "The streets are strewn with them. Times are hard and they will probably get harder. And I think the society and the church are suffering from what they call compassion fatigue. There is only so much you can do. Jerome knows that he could be one of those men."

"He visualized that very powerfully in his painting."

"I would like to buy it," said the superintendent. "But I will not give him the money. Tell him I will donate that money to the Bellevue Mental Hospital. It will be in an amount known only to God, the hospital and myself. I will hang the painting on the wall of this office to remind me that we ought to be doing more for the mentally ill. I recall that the Quakers have done a lot for them. We should do more. Please ask Jerome if he approves of my doing this."

"I will try to see him soon."

"Please give my regards to Mr Jerome Lazarus, such a beautiful religious name! It may be hard for him to see this, but his illness could lead him to his Maker."

We said our goodbyes and I rose to go.

As I left his office I reflected on the wisdom of his solution. No wonder he was the superintendent and I a mere novice-cleric.

I was looking forward to returning to elevated and cool Thankful Hill.

The following evening I decided to visit Jerome Lazarus at his home to discuss the superintendent's proposal to purchase his retablo and donate the money to the Bellevue Hospital. I asked Miss Ina for directions.

"It is easy to find," she said. "Turn left at the church gate and follow the road until you come to the 25th milepost. Turn the big corner after it and you will come to a smaller corner, and at that small corner, on the right side, you will see Jerome's house. You can't miss it for there is a big painting on the wall. It is the only house in Thankful Hill with a painting on the outside."

"Do you know Jerome well?"

"No, Minister. I don't think anybody knows him well. If you ask him a question he will answer, but he will seldom approach you about any matter. When you get there call out his name loud several times for he is a bit hard of hearing, especially if he cannot read your lips. He talks to his relatives mostly. He is a loner."

I left the manse and began walking down the driveway. The road was asphalted and although there were some potholes, I have seen worse on my travels through the hills. On my right I passed a long wall made of cut-stone. Then on my left I peered down into a valley so deep I found myself feeling weak-kneed, for I am slightly altophobic. Further on, still on my left, I noticed a huge hill jutting towards the valley, and I paused to admire the many houses that were built on its sides. Jamaicans are masters of hillside architecture, and it is amazing how they can see a house site where it would be impossible for me to imagine one. On my right I saw the roofs of a collection of houses sloping downhill towards the river. I have never been to this river but would like to go there one of these days. It should be safe for, unlike Belize, Jamaica has no venomous snakes. It seems as if all the poisonous snakes have become the gunmen!

I saw a Rastafarian coming up the road driving a small tethered goat in front of him. He wore a red, black and green tam, a quilt-like overflowing dashiki of some kind, blue jeans and sandals.

"Oi Padre!" he said as soon as he saw me. "Why don't you tell your congregation that there are Black people in the Bible?"

"Some of the characters are believed to be black," I replied, "which is quite plausible given the Bible's geography, but I am not aware that any of the major biblical characters are black. The Bible is a Jewish book and is mainly about Jews. Of course, there have long been black converts to Judaism."

"Jesus was a black man!" he declared.

"You must be a member of the United States Supreme Court! Are you an American?"

"No. I am an African!"

"You are a citizen of which African state?"

"I am an African in exile. We want repatriation now!"

"Good luck!" I said as I resumed walking. I enjoyed reasoning with the Rastas.

Moments later a car pulled up beside me and stopped. Mrs Sonia Walters, our steward and my right-hand woman at the church, was at the wheel. "Can I give you a ride somewhere, Rev. Fernandez?"

"No thanks, Mrs Walters. I need the exercise."

"Okay. Walk good!" She drove off. She and her husband, Major Paul Walters, a disabled ex-serviceman, were becoming good friends and I have spent some pleasant evenings in their beautiful home discussing nearly every subject over a bottle of sherry. Paul was originally from England and was wounded in the war. He occupied his time trying to read the Bible in different languages, with the help of dictionaries.

I passed a grocery shop named "The Daily Bread", the main one in the district. Women were at the counter making purchases, while a group of men were sitting at a table playing dominoes. Children were playing a game in the yard. I greeted them and they responded in a range of expressions, including, "Evening, Parson!", "Hello Minister!", "Fine thank you, Rev.!" and "Bless you, Sir!"

I continued walking.

Miss Ina's directions were perfect. I found myself standing in front of the house which looked more like a shop than a residence, and my eyes were drawn to the huge painting on its outside wall. It was clearly another version of The Good Samaritan theme, apparently a favourite of his. This road to Jericho was clearly not in Palestine, but in rural Jamaica, and in a landscape very similar to Thankful Hill's. This road sloped downhill, and the robbed and wounded traveller, who was more obviously Negroid than the protagonist of the retablo, lay beside a wall made of cut-stone. His beast, a very Jamaican-looking donkey, with its hampers and all, stood on the other side of the road. The Good Samaritan (who was clearly Chinese!) was kneeling beside the wounded man and tending to his wounds. Now I have never seen a Chinese-Jamaican riding a donkey, but it was clear that Jerome had more than cultural verisimilitude in mind. Life is life and art is art, as you would say. And walking down the road, having passed the wounded man, and with a vista of green hills and strip of blue mountain in the distance on their left, were two men. The first who was leading the way, wore a white robe and was clearly the priest, and following him another man also in a white robe but wearing the turban of a revivalist shepherd or captain, representing the Levite. Jerome had Jamaicanized both the landscape and the culture. This was more realistic, and less expressionistic, than the retablo.

I knocked on the locked door but received no response. I remembered Miss Ina's advice and knocked harder and called out his name. After I did that two or three times a door opened and I saw Jerome Lazarus peering out.

"Rev. Fernandez! I didn't expect to see you here!"

"I have news for you about your painting."

"Come in," he said, opening the door wide.

I followed him inside and he pointed to one of the three chairs around a table made of a slice of a giant tree and varnished until it shone. I sat down and noticed that the back door was open, allowing a view of a mountainscape, and casting the light of evening on the numerous paintings that covered the walls, and the sculptures that lined the walls below them.

"Would you like something to drink?" he asked. "I have beers and sodas in the fridge downstairs."

"Sure. I will have a beer."

He went through the door and I heard his footsteps as he went down the outside stairway. I began studying the paintings. Nearly all were of recognizable biblical subjects, including one of a Prodigal Son returning to his mother! There was one of a horrible crucifixion, except that this Jesus is about to be hanged on a gallows (the way the death penalty is carried out here). There was a Last Supper that looked more like a last drink in a rum bar. The sculptures on the floor were mostly the busts of men with troubled and tortured faces reminiscent of Bosch, or some of Leonardo's grotesques. A visit to Jerome Lazarus's studio will be a must when you get here.

I heard his footstep coming up the stairs and he entered with a bottle of beer and a soda for himself. He opened the bottles and handed me my beer which was quite cold. "Cheers!" I said and we clicked bottles.

"You have some amazing paintings here," I said. "Yours is one of the most interesting interpretations of The Good Samaritan that I have ever seen. If you put up a sign which says, 'Paintings for Sale' I am sure tourists on their way to Ocho Rios would stop, look and buy."

"I don't sell my paintings. I sell my carpentry skill, but not my art," he replied.

"But why not?" I asked feeling some disappointment about the superintendent's desire to purchase the retablo. "The people here sell their craftwork to tourists. Why not paintings?"

"My art is a gift from God," he replied. "I once heard of a woman who had the gift of prophecy. She dreamt the numbers that would win the lottery and which horses would win at Caymanas. But she never bought lottery tickets or bet on horses. Her relatives and friends begged her to tell them her dreams, but she kept refusing. Then one of her cousins, the relative she loved most, lost his business and was in deep despair. He begged her to tell him one of her dreams, until finally she relented and told him which horse she saw winning the biggest race for the year at Caymanas. The cousin borrowed money and placed a bet. The horse won! He was on his way to financial recovery. But the woman found that she had lost the gift. She had no more prophetic dreams. I don't want that to happen to me. I invest my art, like the Parable of the Talents (he pointed to one of his paintings), by telling the Bible's stories to the people. I am a bit like you, except that I am an art parson."

"Your painting of "The Good Samaritan" is probably better than any of my sermons on the subject. And people just have to stop and look at it. They don't have to dress up and come to church. As to the retablo, that is between you and God."

"Have you decided what to do with it?"

I told him about the superintendent's proposal.

"That will be fine with me," he said, "for that money will be going to the hospital and not coming to me. And if the superintendent wants to share in my meditation, that will be fine too. Please thank him for me."

I was relieved to hear that and I said so. It seemed to me to be a fitting next step in the retablo's journey. We cannot speculate on any fate which it might have beyond the superintendent's possession. That is beyond both the will of the artist and his spiritual adviser.

It would soon be nightfall, and I wanted to get home on time for supper. I said goodbye to Jerome Lazarus and headed back to the manse.

The following day I called the superintendent on his cellphone and reported on Jerome Lazarus's agreement with his proposal.

"Very good, very good!" he replied. "I will take it home with me this evening. It will have a special place in my meditation room. And please give my regards to Mr Lazarus. I am sure that painting is probably therapeutic for him. It is also a meditative practice. Keep an eye on him."

"I will."

"So long, Rev. Fernandez."

"'Bye Dr Jenkins."

Jerome returned to church the following Sunday. He wore one of his blue suits and seemed well and in good spirits. As usual he sang the hymns fervently, and closely followed the readings. When it was time for the sermon he seemed to be hanging on my every word. I was glad he was there, for it was the example of his retablo that had shifted my mindset from complaining to thanksgiving, and it had influenced my decision to preach the sermon I was about to preach. Of course I did not know that he would be there that Sunday. But coincidentally or non-coincidentally, (you don't believe in coincidences), the New Testament lesson was taken from Luke17:11-19. This is the story of the ten lepers who were healed by Jesus, but only one returned to say thanks. I chose as my text the 17th verse: "And Jesus answering said, Were there not ten cleansed? But where are the nine?" Here is an excerpt from my sermon:

"The freed slaves named this spot Thankful Hill. I do not know if any of my predecessors preached sermons about this important fact. If they did today is my turn. I want to say a few words about those nine lepers who after being healed did not return to thank Jesus, that cleansing of the lepers were ten gifts and blessings. And just as only one leper returned to give thanks, many of us probably give thanks for only one of every ten blessings we receive, that is if we give thanks for any of them at all. Many of us are like those nine ungrateful lepers. Jamaica has many huge, huge problems, but it has some blessings too. While lying in bed last night I reflected on the fact that Jamaicans love to copy the United States of America. We reject their observance of Thanksgiving but enthusiastically embrace their Black Friday. We do not always copy the best things. So last night I identified what I regard as the ten greatest blessings to be found in Jamaica today. I will list them: (1) A fertile and exceedingly beautiful land and excellent climate. An agricultural expert once told me that except for wheat (it doesn't get cold enough here for this crop), nearly every other crop can be grown in Jamaica. Yet we grow little and import most of our food. The climate is mostly benevolent, except for rare hurricanes and earthquakes. Where on God's earth is more beautiful than the drive along the coast from St Thomas to Portland? (2) The farmers and craft-makers. I am referring to the people who grow the food in our rich soil. And the people who make things from what is grown, like our straw-workers right here in Thankful Hill. (3) The Food. Like most people I am partial to the food of my own country. But there are certain Jamaican foods that I am coming to love. For me there is no coffee better than Blue Mountain Coffee. No fruits seem to me to be tastier than Jamaican Julie mangoes and starapples. And I cannot go to Mandeville without stopping at the Yam Park for roast yam and saltfish. (4) Parliamentary democracy. Jamaicans love to blame and curse their politicians, and God knows some of them deserve it. But Jamaica is one of the few predominantly black countries with an unbroken history of parliamentary democracy. This is not something to sneeze at. We are consistently ranked as a country with one of the highest levels of press freedom in the world. Our elections are mostly free and fair. I don't think there are any political prisoners in our jails. We have not yet produced a vicious dictator. (5) Tourism. It is often overlooked, but this is one of the areas in which Jamaica has achieved internationally recognized excellence. It has innovators in tourism who are second to none. (6) The educators. One of the most remarkable facets of the country's history has been the enormous rehabilitation project, through education, which began right after slavery and continues to this day. It has been a collaborative project involving the descendants of both the enslavers and the enslaved. And the aspect of the church of which I am most proud (I am also ashamed of many aspects of it too) is the role it has played as one of the educators in both spiritual and secular matters. (7) The innovators. This does not strike me as a particularly innovative culture, for mimicry seems to be more the norm, so I am especially grateful for all the people who have invented things. Like Dr T. P. Lecky for developing the Jamaica Hope breed of cattle. Like Charles Jackson, I bet you have never heard of him, the man who is credited with developing the ortanique fruit in Manchester. Like the agriculturalists who invented the Bodles Globe pumpkin, and the manufacturers who invented Pikapeppa Sauce and Tia Maria. I am thinking of the innovators in the field of music who have enriched the experiences of our island and the world with their original musical compositions. I am thinking of innovators in the fields of business and commerce. I am thinking too of the social and political innovators who created social institutions like Jamaica Welfare, the National Housing Trust, The National Insurance Scheme, The Urban Development Corporation, The Jamaica Festival Song Competition and too many to list. I must include the innovators in literature, dance, architecture, the visual arts, fashion, media and software. (8) Functionaries. I am not sure this is the right word but I can't think of a better one. I am referring to all the people who implement the ideas of the thinkers and innovators. They include civil servants, the police, soldiers, nurses and doctors, without whom the affairs of everyday life could not be carried out. (9) Charitable organizations. There is a streak to do good to others here, which is perhaps most noticeable in your Labour Day voluntary activities. Nearly all our churches, including our own, are engaged in some form of charitable work. But they are all falling very short. Only recently I had occasion to notice the large number of homeless people, including the mentally ill, on the streets of Kingston. We need leaders who can put the spirit of Labour Day into social transformation.(10) I conclude with the entertainers. These are the artistes and sportsmen and women who excite and entertain us, who unite us, who move our emotions and challenge us to look at ourselves, sometimes with tears and sometimes with laughter.

"I shall avoid the error of the lepers by giving thanks for only one of these ten blessings. If I do Jesus will ask me 'Where are the nine?' I want to challenge you to draw up your own list of ten blessings tonight when you go to bed, just before you fall asleep. And give thanks for all of them! I must keep reminding you. Don't let Jesus have to come to your bedside and ask, 'Where are the nine?' I am thinking of putting a Thankfull Hill Sunday on our annual calendar, and I will invite your input. Where are the nine? Today the nine of us will say to Jesus, 'We are here, and thank you, Jesus!'"

We concluded with the singing of the Methodist Anthem, and my own favourite hymn: 'And can it be that I Should Gain'. It is a hymn of thanksgiving for Jesus. I can't recall ever seeing Jerome sing with such zest. We raised the roof of the church with that one.

After the service I greeted each member of the congregation at the exit. There were many good natured and humorous emphases on the words 'thank you' as I shook hands with them. When it was Jerome's turn he had a twinkle in his eyes when he said, "I am glad you didn't leave out the artists. Your sermon was a retablo."

"You knew the meaning of the word before you heard it," I replied.

He smiled and went down the steps.

By now this letter is nearly as big as a parcel. Writing it has filled my lonely nights while I think of you. And of all the stories I have experienced since I have been here, this is the one that has made me think of you most, and the one I feel like sharing in the greatest detail. An artist's life is never easy, and I know that you struggle with a lot there too. I look forward to hearing more about some of them when you write next.

My love and care surround you.

As ever.

Peter

Lively Up Yourself

(Article from The Jamaica Sun)

The residents of *Mt Carlos in St Andrew woke* up to a surprise last Ash Wednesday. There was an art exhibition mounted in the square titled "Lively up Yourself". The paintings were by Ras We-dren (real name Ainsley Williams), a student at the School of Art who was born in that district, and who had spent a year there painting its way of life while on a sabbatical funded by a grant from the Canadian Postcolonial Development Agency.

I arrived there at 10:00 am and was welcomed by the youthful, dreadlocked Ras We, as he is affectionately called. A slender young man with gentle, thoughtful eyes, he turned and introduced me to Miss Selena Edwards, his fellow student and assistant. The square was lined with paintings mounted on bamboo railings on the western and northern sides, allowing space for the occasional traffic that from time to time passed through the quiet rural community, and that was regulated at both ends by two policemen.

"Why the title 'Lively up Yourself'?" I asked him. He had said a little about this title when he called the paper, but I wanted to hear more.

"I was thinking of the Black African view that a work of art is an embodiment of a vital force or spirit that is released by dancing. That is why there will be a dance here tonight after the show. I have adopted this view of art as my own philosophy. Rastafari played an important role in Bob Marley's outlook, and his song 'Lively up Yourself' seems to me to be in keeping with the release of that spirit in art. I also want the entire event to be an example of what Americans call a 'Happening'. It is art within art."

"Sounds mystical to me."

"Mysticism is a part of virtually every religion, and this is also true of Rastafari."

"Now tell me about your chosen name: 'Ras We-dren'."

"You have 'Brethren' and 'Sistren'. So I have chosen the collective, 'We-dren'."

"Got it."

Music was blaring from a boom-box on the table in the bamboo booth in the middle of the eastern row of paintings, and in front of an old, closed shop. The opening ceremony would be held there later in the afternoon. Selena Edwards was putting a maroon tablecloth on the table. A few residents were walking around and examining the paintings.

"Desmond, a local carpenter, made the bamboo railings for me," continued Ras We. "The paintings are all acrylics on canvas. Let me give you a tour."

I passed GCE 'O' Level Art and do not claim to be an expert, but this was partly why my editor had chosen me to cover this show. He thought the event was quite extraordinary, something he had never heard of before, and since the paper was committed to promoting the island's culture, he felt it was important that we should cover it.

I found some of the pieces very moving. These included Hill Song, a portrayal of the landscape that was the home of the show, done in energetic vertical brushstrokes of greens and blues; "Yam Farmer", a rearview of a man digging yam-hills; "Market Prelude" that showed three higglers in evening light packing produce into crocus bags while waiting for the arrival of truck; "Mento Composition With Corn", a semi-abstract piece showing corncobs with the grains showing, arranged into a pattern; "The Shepherd's Dream", a fantasy piece that showed a Revivalist leader, in white turban and robe, sleeping in a garden of local plants and flowers, while above him is the dream he is having of an Afro-Jamaican heaven; "Ghost of the Canefield" that showed a woman in plantation-style dress hurrying beside a canefield at nightfall, and caught in the headlights of a passing automobile; and "Political Tribalism", the biggest piece in the show, that showed two rolling calves, with their horns locked in a brutal conflict, their eyes red and glowing.

I complimented the artist, but he only nodded with a thoughtful look in his eyes.

"Let me introduce you to some people," he said.

I met Maas Tim, the rotund and cheerful curry-goat cook who was 'stirring-it-up' a huge Dutch-pot over a wood fire at the northeastern corner of the square. "His wife cannot get him to boil an egg at home," said Ras We, "but he is the most famous curry-goat cook in the parish. They hire him for fairs and weddings. He is also a famous storyteller, and if you have time for a few Anansi stories this is the man."

"I going to hire him as my agent," said Maas Tim. I later had the opportunity to sample his specialty of goat with white rice, boiled green bananas, washed down with a beer, and it was so good I advised him to give or sell his recipe to a restaurant in Kingston or the north coast. We were joined by Desmond, the carpenter, a wiry light-skinned man with gold teeth. "I bet you never did anything like this before," I said to him.

"Not in my wildest dreams," he replied. "Every day me see Ainsley going around the place looking, and drawing, but me never think it would come to anything like this. Some people thought he was mad."

"I should tell them about Vincent Van Gogh, a real mad and great artist," said Ras We with a chuckle. Then we went to the booth and he introduced me to Wenty P, as he called himself, the young man with a wide grin, the selector who was playing the music. Ras We said, "I told him to play all kinds of Jamaican music: folk, mento, ska, rock steady, reggae, dancehall, gospel, hymns, the works, interspersed with our Marley theme song."

The number of persons viewing the paintings had increased and I asked a few of them about their reactions to the paintings and the event.

"It is a big surprise to me," said a woman with missing front teeth and who wore a white frock. "Me never see anything like this in Mt Carlos before. Or hear anything about anything like it. Mi grandfather say they used to have an animal market here in the old days. When me was a pickney dem used to have film show. And a shopkeeper used to own a sound system. But nothing like this."

"Image! Image! Image! All graven images!" said a woman with natural hair who stared at me fiercely through her dark-brown frames of her spectacles. "Some a dem look so real dem make me feel afraid, as if there is a kind of life in dem. But I give him this—de boy wittify fi true."

An old man with grey hair and who wore jeans and sandals, said, "To tell you de truth, a never expected anything like this to come out of this district. It is all so strange and new to me. I am still trying to make sense of it. But I hear that these paintings can cost thousands of dollars. Tourists and banks buy them. I saw some in the waiting room of my doctor in Kingston. So this boy could go far. I am proud of the youngster. Most of the young people grow up, get their education and leave. Ainsley brought something back to us. Some of us going to remember these paintings for the rest of our lives. I can't put my finger on it, but I think something extraordinary is happening here today. And whatever it might mean, I thank him for it."

I spoke with a little boy. "Mi can draw too, you know," he said. "But is the first time me ever seen anybody draw things me can recognize, like the man digging the yam-hills, the waterfall where we bathe on Sunday mornings, and boys like me playing gigs. So now me know dat big people can draw too."

Some of the people who entered the square were on their way to various errands. All stopped to look around at the paintings. A farmer who had a goat on a rope led the animal around on his tour of the pieces. A man burst out laughing in front of a piece sowing a couple roasting yams on a coal-stove. The man with a hoe on his shoulder, contemplating the painting of the fighting rolling calves, looked as if he himself could one day be the subject of a painting by Ras We-dren. A minibus entered the square, stopped and disgorged its passengers, and continued on its journey. All the disembarked passengers stopped to look at the works of art before continuing to their homes on the hillsides that sloped around the square.

By mid-afternoon, dignitaries began arriving for the opening ceremony. Desmond assisted the policemen in directing them to parking on a sideroad. Each official was welcomed by Ras We-dren and escorted to their seats in the booth. The ceremony started just after 4:00 pm.

The chairman was Mr Ansel Reid, principal of the school. He welcomed the fair-sized gathering. He said he had not taught Ainsley 'Ras We-dren' Williams, who had attended before his time, but he was pleased to see one of its former pupils on the verge of tackling the world of Jamaican art. Unlike many educated citizens of the country, he had shown that his home district was not only a place to come from, but a place to return to in some significant way. Art could help to build communities, and he planned to ask the budding artist to advise him on how his school could contribute to this. He confessed that they did not even have an art programme but that Ras We-dren really energised the district of Mt Carlos today.

He was clapped and cheered.

"Hear! Hear! Bread and pear!" a man shouted.

Dr Howard Kerr, head of the Canadian agency that had granted Ras We-dren the award to carry out this project, and who had come to the island to share in its completion, said what a joy if was for him to finally visit the island of Harry Belafonte and Bob Marley, and to hear their music not in his wintry home in Winnipeg, but in the kind of community from which this music sprang, and how much he enjoyed driving up into those beautiful and salubrious hills that deserved to be as famous as the island's beaches. He had seen many art exhibitions, but never one in a remote village in a Third World country. He was happy that his organization could help to make such a thing possible. He congratulated Ras We-dren on his remarkable creativity and enterprise. Perhaps he could spearhead a school of Jamaican Mountain Art the way artists in his own country had made their Prairie Art famous. After its premier at Mt Carlos, a beginning that Ras We-dren had insisted on, the exhibition would be mounted in the gallery of the School of Art in Kingston, and later hopefully to the headquarters of his organization in Canada. The paintings would be sold to help fund the rest of Ras We-dren's education. Part of the proceeds would also go to assisting art education programmes in Jamaican primary schools. "Mt Carlos to the World!" he concluded to warm applause.

The next speaker was Dr Tanya Archer, the principal of the School of Art. She said the mission of the school was not only to train artists in its studios for the advancement of the spiritual, social and economic life of the country, but to do so by also taking art to the people. It was for that reason why they were pleased when Mr Williams, Ras We-dren, applied to the Canadian Development Agency to do this project. They were very pleased to see the success he had made of it, and they looked forward to hosting the show at the school. The other students would learn from and be inspired by Ras We-dren's work.

"Shakespeare said that art is a mirror that artists hold up to a society so that it can see itself reflected.

And you all know that when you look into a mirror you see things about yourself that you both know and did not know. So today Ras We-dren has held up such a mirror before Mt Carlos, and it is for you to detect in these pieces both what you know and did not know about yourselves, and to think about both. So, Big-Up Ras We!" she concluded to warm applause.

Selena Edwards then escorted Ras We-dren's grandmother, Mrs Eugenia Williams, fondly known as 'Mama Willie', to her speaking position at the centre-front of the booth. She wore a white head-tie and white dress.

"Is me grow him," she said to great applause. "Him mother and father deh a foreign. It is hard to believe dat this little suck-finger boy do a thing like this in the Mt Carlos square today. (Laughter) Him lively up the place fe true. To think me up here with all these big-shot people. Mi heart full. (Cheers) Him is not God so him cannot breathe the breath of life, but when I look at these pictures some of them look so alive I have to admit that there is some kind of life in them. What that is I cannot say. I only went as far a third class at school. But if God make Adam, Adam should make something for himself too. (Cheers) But I know that Ainsley, or whatever him choose to call himself these days, must never forget that he did not give himself these gifts. And him have a gift, that is clear. That gift must come from a higher power. (Applause) I have only one request. Him can take these pictures to wherever he wants—Kingston, Canada, anywhere. But there is one of them that must come back to me to me for me to hang and to keep in my little house here in Mt Carlos. And I am not talking about the ugly one he did of me. I am talking the one he did of himself. That one must stay here to remind me of how he grow up, went to school, and became what he did here today. (Applause) It was nice but at the same time not easy having him stay in mi house for a whole year while he was painting these things. But to tell you the truth, me I will also be glad to get all these fandangles outa mi house. (Laughter) So mi grandson turn big artist. Ainsley, all I want to say is, walk good mi love. And may good duppy always walk with you."

They gave her a standing ovation.

Ras We-dren spoke next.

"I am a painter not an elocutionist, so I prefer to let my paintings do the talking. But I wish to thank all the persons who helped to make this event happen." He gave a long list that left out only the dogs that ate the bones of the curry goat. "Dr Kerr has challenged me to lead a Blue Mountain group of painters in this country. I promise that I will begin by trying to become the best painter of our mountains that I can be, and then try to see what I and others can do later. I will discuss with Mr Reid the possibility of my putting on a slide show of Jamaican art the school. (Applause) Mamma Willie, that painting will be yours to keep. (Applause) And even if my painting of you is ugly, you are not. In my eyes you are the most beautiful woman in this district. (Applause) Of course, we all know she was only making one of her frequent self-deprecating remarks. After the dance tonight, the final enjoyment of ourselves, the paintings will be left in the square overnight. I want them to commune with the spirit of this place, including the ancestors, those now living and the unborn. I want the moon to cross the sky and look down at them. Tomorrow a van will come and take them to Kingston."

"Nobody nah tief dem!" someone shouted from the crowd.

"The praedial larcenists not tiefing art yet?" Ras We-dren fired back.

Than he added, "I would like to conclude by modifying the words of Bob Marley: 'Philosophy of art flying through my head, light as a feather heavy as lead!'"

He sat down to loud applause.

The Hon. Jasmine Wedderburn, Minister of Culture, had the last word.

"I have been travelling all over the island attending cultural events, but never to one like this. And it had to come out of Mt Carlos. (Cheers) We are perceived mostly as a music and sports country, but I hope the time will come when we will speak as powerfully with our paint brushes and chisels as we now do with our voices and feet. This is a challenge for young men and women like Ras We-dren and Selena Edwards. And from what I am seeing today, the world should watch out! What has happened here today should be seen as not only an art exhibition but a metaphor of what can come out of our rural communities. It is no accident that so many of the movers and shakers in our society, in all fields, including culture, came from rural communities such as Mt Carlos. Please teach that to your children, Mr Reid. Never let your art students forget that, Dr Archer. Ras We-dren, you have made Mama Willie and all the people of this community proud. Marcus Garvey said that art is the highest expression of human intelligence and genius. Let us heed his words. On behalf of the government and people of Jamaica, I congratulate all of you."

She concluded by listing some of the cultural achievements of her administration so far. She was warmly applauded as she took her seat.

As Ras We-dren began giving the dignitaries a final tour of the exhibition, I prepared to leave. I joined the convoy of departing cars as one of the policemen guided us out of the square. Wenty P had just turned up the volume of the music. The last thing I noticed was Desmond and a woman in a red dress dancing with great vigour.

PAUL GREENFIELD, STAFF REPORTER/PHOTOGRAPHER

Something Is Gone

I *was in the art studio preparing for my tutorial* with Professor Tom Bernstein, who insisted that his students call him 'Bernie'.

I put my two most recent paintings on two easels side by side. Then I stepped back to look at them.

On the left was a full-view portrait of a man carrying a big bundle of breadfruits on his head. I had titled it 'A Breadfruit Man'. On the right was a portrayal of a section of the wall of a ruined building with the words THE HILLVIEW GROCERY once written in red paint, but now barely visible on the bluish, smoke-stained wall. I had titled it 'Ruined Handwriting'. I studied the two pieces carefully. 'A Breadfruit Man' was based on memory from my childhood in Jamaica. 'Ruined Handwriting' was based on a photograph of the remains of my aunt's little country shop that had been broken into seventeen times and burnt to the ground on the eighteenth attack by political activists during the war that ended democratic socialism at the end of the 1970s. The sign on the wall had been written by me, at my aunt's request, while I was a schoolboy.

Bernie entered the studio. He was tall and slender, mostly bald but with a red beard, and he wore a red T-shirt and blue jeans. He painted mostly abstract pieces, and one I had seen had red ovals of varying sizes on a white background. He was well-known in the art world of New York.

"Hi Frank. Let's see what you have been up to."

We pulled up two stools and sat side by side as we examined the paintings.

"Tell me about the one on the left." He liked hearing you talk about your work before he offered his comments.

"It is based on my memory of my cousin Ced. He was my mother's nephew. He inherited a piece of land from his grandfather. It was in a deep valley beside a river and he cultivated it with much enthusiasm. I remember once seeing him coming up the path from his field, with a huge bundle of breadfruits he had just harvested from his trees. I tried to capture his pride in his labour, and his satisfaction with his harvest."

"You captured that very well. What else about him should I look for in this picture?"

"He was very attached to my parents. He caught crayfish in the river and brought them to my mother to make soup. He brought us mangoes from his trees. When my father became an invalid, he visited him often and did errands for him. They watched TV together. He loved cricket and one of his greatest pleasures was to see batsmen hit sixes and fours."

"Any personality quirks?"

"He was so kind to us, yet his favourite movies were those that showed the crucifixion of Jesus. And while he enjoyed seeing beautiful strokes in cricket, he once chided me for weeding my mother's garden, since, he said, flowers cannot be eaten! He regretted not being able to eat flowers, yet he was a famous maker of ice cream. The Chinese make tea from flowers so they are edible. We could say he had a discordant aesthetic."

"I am not yet seeing that in his portrait. Paint it!"

"I will try," I said with a laugh. "His devotion to my father was remarkable. I don't know why. My father was famous for his generosity and he may have done something for Ced that Ced never forgot. He addressed my father only by his nickname, 'Shorty' and he was the only person I knew who did that. The day after my father died, he came to our home early saying that my father had appeared to him in a dream and told him that the boards for his coffin were kept under the house. He found them, dragged them out and took them to the carpenter."

"Rembrandt could put a character's life and soul in the expression in his eyes."

"I have seen some of them."

"There is no harm in aiming that high, for it would pull out the best in you."

"It is good for a light-heavyweight boxer to spar with a heavyweight."

"Exactly."

"You are unlikely to see an image like this in New York, so I should probably tell you a little about breadfruits. In the South Sea Islands they were called the fruit of kings. During a famine it was brought to the West Indies by Captain Bligh to feed slaves. You may have heard about the famous Mutiny on the Bounty. Well, that ship was the first attempt at taking them to Jamaica. The second ship succeeded. But the slaves were reluctant to eat this strange fruit. Eventually it became a loved staple and is eaten boiled, roasted or fried. The plant is very resilient and there is a Jamaican proverb that says, 'The more you chop down breadfruit root is the more it spring'. After the mutiny, Bligh was put on a ship and sent out to sea. He managed to reach Timor and made his way back to England. He tried again and succeeded. So Bligh was himself a kind of breadfruit man in his persistence, and his belief in the power of new suckers springing up. I want to portray Ced as the strong and resilient man that he was."

"Did he have a family?"

"Yes. His wife ran a cold-supper shop in the square at Mt Carlos. They had four children. Both he and his wife have passed away. I have no present contact with their children."

"You are right that I have never seen an image like this."

"So, let me tell you some more. Between the fruits and his head, to relieve the pressure, is a coiled, dry banana leaf that is called a cotta. Carrying loads on the head is an African retention in Jamaica. Right now, there is a lot of scientific research being done on the breadfruit. They say there is a species that has more protein then the soya bean. The breadfruit could help fight hunger and famine in the world."

"I am learning a lot from you, Frank. Now let me say a few things aesthetic to earn my salary. When I look at this painting I am reminded of Georgia O' Keefe's view that it is by seeing and emphasizing the abstraction seen in the real object that distinguishes a painting from a photograph. I see a lot of possibilities for that here, in the interrelation between the breadfruit — spheres, and each fruit a unique object. And in the patterns on the surface of the fruits; in the harmony between the geometry of the breadfruits and Ced's face and clothing. All this is contrasted with the atmospheric effect of the negative shapes, which I assumed aim at capturing the light of the morning. One more thing. Cezanne made the apple a famous icon in western art. You could become the Cezanne of the breadfruit. Did Gauguin paint breadfruits? He probably did but I can't recall. Here is a challenge for you."

"I can see that you have a lot of confidence in your students!"

"Of course. They must become better artists than I am. Or I will have failed. Now let us turn to the other painting."

"They are connected but I will say more about that later. This one is harder to talk about. I must first tell you about the woman behind it. She was Aunt Dora who was also my godmother. As the eldest daughter in her family, unmarried and childless, she became a mother-figure for all of us. After she left school she opened a stall in a market in Kingston. With the money earned she returned to Mt Carlos and opened a little shop. As it prospered she bought a piece of land on a hill near the square and built a bigger shop on it. It was designed and built by a master carpenter, an in-law, and it was the finest shop for miles around. I was a schoolboy when she opened it, and knowing about my artistic leanings, she asked me to write the name of the shop, THE HILLVIEW GROCERY on the front wall. The name was appropriate because from that spot you could see many valleys, hills and mountains, even parts of the famous Blue Mountains in the distance. You could see the sun rise, cross the sky, and set in the west. You could see the nearby Baptist church whose members were some of her main customers. I was proud to be a useful artist, so using the instruments in my geometry set, I made and painted the sign. I was proud of my work and happy to help my godmother.

"After I left school I worked with an optician in Kingston and learned the trade. During the turmoil of democratic socialism on the island in the 1970s my boss migrated and quickly filed for me. I joined him here in New York. His business did well and I am still working for his company, and taking this art course one evening per week.

"I got married to Taba who is from the Philippines. She is an architect. We both love the tropics and got the idea of going to live in Jamaica, now that democratic socialism is over. I would acquire a piece of land from my father and we would build a self-sufficient house on it, with solar energy and harvested rain water. We would do organic farming. We could get jobs in Kingston and commute.

"I made my first trip back to the island since I left. The flight was delayed and I arrived at the Norman Manley Airport late at night. A taximan charged me a fortune to take me to Mt Carlos. The following morning my mother welcomed me with a wonderful breakfast of ackee and saltfish, roast breadfruit, big ripe tangerines and homemade coffee. You should go to Jamaica and try that food sometime. Over breakfast I put my proposal to my mother and father.

"'Don't come back here!' said my mother. 'Because we are a little better off, they have been after us all our lives. They cut out the tongue of one of my father's horses. They connived with one of my brothers to steal parts from the engine of his truck and wrecked the vehicle. And you should go talk to Aunt Dora to see what they did to her.'

"My father was quiet but as a carpenter he was intrigued by the idea of a self-sufficient house and wanted to hear more about it. He said I should listen to what my mother had to say, but that he would not advise me one way or the other. He would let me have the land if I really wanted it, but he preferred to let me make up my own mind.

"After breakfast I set off to visit Aunt Dora. The ruins of the shop that was so much a part of my childhood, shocked me. It was one of the saddest things I have ever seen. I searched the ruins and found the remains of the sign I had written on it. It was now smoke-stained and covered with grime. As an artist you know how we artists feel about the works we create. When I was a boy, I liked drawing in my exercise books, but that sign was my first piece of public art. It may look like a simple thing to some people, but not to me. I have always been some kind of artist—I am now into designing spectacles—and this painting course is a step towards becoming a better artist. I took a photograph of the damaged sign and brought it back with me.

"Aunt Dora told me more about her trauma when I continued down the road to the old family home where she was now living with a sister. She told me about the numerous break-ins and the final act of arson.

"'And as if that wasn't enough,' she said, 'they came here night after night and threatened us with guns. And calling me a capitalist. What the hell is a capitalist? They never taught me that word at school. I never heard it until this socialism thing rise up.'

'Was the shop insured?' I asked her.

'No. And I reinvested all my profits back into it. I tried my best to help myself and the family and anyone in the district who I could help. Even Jojo, a man I used to give lunch to everyday, turned against me. He hit me with a piece of board and I had to be taken to the doctor. I was lucky to escape major injury, the doctor said.'

'So how are you managing now?'

'I sell things from here.' She pointed to sacks and crates of sodas on the floor of the dining room.

"I returned to New York and reported on my visit to Taba. We agreed not to go any further with this plan. And here am I trying to make a painting out of a photograph of my sign."

Bernie was leaning forward with his chin on his hands and contemplating the painting.

"That is quite a story Frank. I remember reading about some of that turmoil in Jamaica in the newspapers here. My girlfriend and I cancelled a planned vacation there. But I have never met anyone directly affected by it."

"A lot of Jamaicans live here. They call New York Kingston 21, 22, or something like that."

"This painting is stirring a lot of thoughts in me. In the first place the link between the image and the word is a long and complex one. The Chinese are masters of this since their calligraphy is a kind of picture-writing, and it is a highly developed and very complex art form. Combining calligraphy with visual realistic images is very much part of their tradition. Of course, you also have calligrammes, poems arranged to visually resemble their subject matter. You may want to look up the calligraphic painting that influenced abstract expressionism, a movement that was once very big in this city.

"In the Western tradition, Paul Klee has done interesting things combining letters, including poems, into paintings. Cy Tombly wrote classical poetry on his canvasses. Some complain that this makes paintings too literary. Its meaning should not depend too much on the meaning of words or the story behind it, as yours does. The visual images should speak for themselves. So, I am suggesting that you make the visual images tell most of the story. Put some cracks in the wall, and have some plants growing out of them to convey the idea that this is a dead grocery-shop. Perhaps your title could be, 'The Dead Shop'. It is no longer a centre of village commerce with a magnificent view."

"I like that idea of a dead shop and I will work on it."

"How did your Aunt Dora manage?"

"She got dementia. And they say they never saw her happier. She escaped the sorrows of the island into the cheerful blackout of her senility."

"And what is the connection between these two pieces?"

"'A Breadfruit Man' is a reminder of the Jamaica of my youth. 'The Dead Shop', if I call it that, destroyed many of those pleasant memories. Jamaica lost something between 'A Breadfruit Man' and 'The Dead Shop', and I am trying hard to see if I can identify what that was and why it happened. In this painting I am trying to use my art to transform my ruin into a temple I can pray in."

Bernie made a sound of understanding in his throat but said nothing. It was the sound of a man who knew he communicated best with the visual images he made.

SOMETHING IS GONE

"You have quite a task there," he finally said. "And are you sure you will never go back there?"

"Only if, like its breadfruits, it springs some new shoots."

Bernie rose to go.

"You are doing well, Frank. Keep going."

I watched him as he walked out of the studio.

I sat for a long time studying the paintings and trying to imagine what I needed to do to improve them. The ideas would come while lying in bed beside Taba.

CPSIA information can be obtained
at www.ICGtesting.com
Printed in the USA
LVHW040931230422
716898LV00004B/10